Til Blood Do Us Part

Marianna Buffolino

ISBN: 979-8-9897821-4-7

In the shadows where love and danger entwine, villians discover that desire can ignite a fire even in the coldest of hearts.

Author's Note

Hello dear reader,

This book contains darker themes including pillory, forced punishment, dub-con, forced voyeurism, cheating MMC, off page rape, murder of a parent and sibling.

Please be mindful of your triggers before you proceed.

Thanks for reading!

Prologue

"Mama? Papochka?"

Walking through the foyer of my parents' home, there is an odd silence.

"Mama? Papochka?" I call again with a trembling voice as I scan the ornate hallway that is lined with family portraits that now feel like accusing eyes.

Making my way to the living room, the grand chandelier flickers, casting eerie shadows against the marble floor. Furniture lies overturned, glass scattered across the floor like fallen stars. The air is thick with an overwhelming sense of loss and violence. Then, I see them.

My parents lie motionless on the ground, necks split wide open, while their bodies are surrounded by the remnants of what has been a seemingly peaceful family life. A scream catches in my throat as I stumble back, my breath hitching as the reality of the situation crashes over me like a wave.

"You must be Lana," a deep voice rumbles from the shadows, freezing me in place. Emerging into the dim light is Adrian Sokolov, the son of Moscow's bratva leader and my family's rival, his presence commanding and terrifying. His white shirt is stained with blood, clinging to his body, showing his sculpted muscles that are decorated with tattoos. For a man who spent 5 years locked in Russia's most brutal prison, he has wasted no time in making his name known within the first few weeks as a free man by eliminating any rival or competitor within Moscow and the surrounding cities.

"What have you done?" I gasp, tears blurring my vision as I wipe them away angrily. "You monster!"

He steps forward, his gaze unyielding, a cruel smirk playing on his lips while his piercing gray eyes hold an unsettling depth of danger.

"Your mother begged me to spare her life. Will you do the same?"

His footsteps, as he approaches me, send waves of panic through my veins. He would terrify the devil himself, make the boogeyman look like a saint. The room somehow fills with more men, and I know the end of my life is here. Adrian stands tall, towering over me, his dark hair tousled yet impeccably styled and framing his face, which is both striking and intimidating. His skin is a perfect canvas, accentuating the sharp angles of his jawline and high cheekbones. There is a raw intensity in the way he moves that shows he's always in control on the surface, waiting for the moment to let out the ruthlessness, to manipulate and destroy anyone or anything in his way.

A tear slides down my face with a sad attempt at a threat. "My husband will avenge us."

"Who do you think helped plan this?" His smile is laced with a sinister undertone, revealing a set of perfectly white teeth that hint at a darker nature lurking beneath the surface.

"He wouldn't," I reply, raising my voice.

With a calmness, he snaps his fingers, and someone comes into view. That man, being my husband, stands beside Adrian with his head held high.

"It's not personal, my love. It's just business."

My eyes widen at my husband's words. "Beau, how could you? My father gave you everything." He has become the son my father never had.

Without remorse, Beau simply shrugs. "Everything but power, Lana. I took his advice. Don't rely on someone giving you what you want—you just need to take it."

"Te mudak! *You asshole*," I yell as though my life isn't on the line and ignore the frightening men surrounding me.

"Lana, your father was being too stubborn. Pairing with the Sokolov family is the right move," Beau seems convinced of this as he speaks the words. "Adrian has already removed any threat here in Moscow. Soon enough, he will rule Russia, and we will be by his side."

"That wasn't your choice to make," I say, seething through my teeth. "So, what now?"

The sudden crack of the gunshot echoes in the confined space, drowning out every sound—the gasp of my breath and the pounding of my heart. I watch in horror as the side of Beau's head explodes like a grotesque canvas splattering paint. Red-gray matter is smeared wildly across the walls, leaving an unnerving, gruesome artwork of violence. A thick cloud of gunpowder mixes with the metallic scent of blood hanging in the air, creating a suffocating atmosphere.

My body feels heavy, as if anchored to the ground by an unseen force, and all I can do is breathe erratically, struggling to comprehend the scene before me. Adrian turns, his steely gaze locked onto me with a chilling calm as he holds his gun. The weapon, a PB pistol, now aimed unwaveringly at my forehead, seems like an extension of his will—cold, menacing, and utterly devoid of remorse. The horror of Beau's fate mingles with the primal urge to survive, leaving me paralyzed in despair.

"So, what now?" His deep, smooth voice seems to be capable of soothing words and chilling threats, and I'm not sure which is being implied here. It seems when he speaks, it's as if every syllable is weighed with intent, leaving those who listen hanging on his every word, even when they know they should be wary. This makes him both alluring and terrifying, an embodiment of the fine line between charm and menace, beauty and danger. Barely able to keep eye contact with such a daunting man, I am afraid to answer.

"If you want to kill me, then do it already." My body trembles with fear.

Adrian points the gun at my head, seemingly eager to pull the trigger. The gold ring around his pinky is like his crown. This will be another medallion for him. We Petrovi will just be another rival family's brutal slaughter. They say Adrian went in a decent man and returned as a savage animal.

Before I can meet my fate, one of his men walks up to him to hand him a cellphone as he whispers something into Adrian's ear. Taking the phone from the man, with an irate tone, he answers with a sharp, "What." He goes silent, his body rigid, his knuckles white from his grip on the phone, then looks at me before ending the call.

In a short breath, his massive hand wraps around my neck, restricting my air flow as he lifts me onto my feet and pulls me close to his face.

"You're one lucky little bitch," he seethes.

Letting go of my neck, I gasp for air. "If you're going to kill me, just do it."

Letting out a huff of annoyance, his next words haunt me. "Unfortunately, I'll have to marry you instead."

My heart races, a tempest of emotions swirling within me—rage, grief, disbelief. "I'd rather die than be tied down to a monster like you."

"Trust me, I'd rather you be dead, but you're more valuable alive." Pulling at his collar as though it is suffocating him, I notice his hand has a skull tattoo that is equally as scary as he is. "You'll need to be my alibi."

"I'm not covering up this mess for you."

An evil laugh spills out of his mouth, his tone almost conversational. "You can die here, alongside your precious family, or you can marry me. Join the Sokolov family and secure your family's legacy in a different way."

Confused, I angrily look at him. "I wouldn't have to secure my legacy if you hadn't taken it from me."

"I'm offering you a chance to survive," he counters, his eyes narrowing. "It's a one-time opportunity. In this world, strength is power. Marrying me means protection, influence. You could help rebuild what's left of your family's name. Refuse, and I'll leave you to the wolves."

"The wolves?" I'm not sure if he is speaking literally or figuratively.

His expression darkens, the predatory gleam in his eyes more pronounced. "Take me out of the picture, and you think your father's enemies won't come for you? He has a long list of rivals, both criminal and political. They will make you suffer in ways unimaginable."

My mind goes blank. He is right. Growing up with criminals, I know you can only trust someone as far as you can throw them.

"What do you get out of marrying me?" I ask as I am

curious how sparing my life benefits him. "That alibi excuse isn't enough for a man like you to spare me."

"What do you know about what kind of man I am?" he shoots back.

I fall silent.

"Ivan, bring Ms. Petrova to my estate." With that, he turns on his heel.

A man double his size stands beside me as I watch Adrian and the rest of his men leave me standing amidst the wreckage of my life, the gravity of his ultimatum hanging heavy in the air. As the door clicks shut behind them, I sink to my knees, tears streaming down my face as I grip my parents' cold hands, the weight of my world crashing down around me. I am alone now, faced with an impossible choice, and the shadow of the Sokolov family looms like a dark cloud over my future.

Chapter 1

Adrian

"What's taking her so long?"

"Well, she did just find her parents with their throats cut open."

I glance up at Ivan, my go-to man for everything, the one who handles the real dirty work. We met in prison and instantly knew by his savage behavior that he would fit perfectly into my bratva. The first time I came across Ivan was when he was pulling a man's eyeball out of his socket.

"Did she make a fuss when you took her to the west wing?" I sit down, leaning back on my chair, holding a cup half full of vodka.

"She hasn't said a word." Ivan takes a shot, then pours himself another. "How long do you plan on keeping her as your wife?"

"Once we marry, she's my property, which means all her father's assets become mine. After that, do what you want with her." Gulping the shot of vodka, I savor the burning sensation of it traveling down my throat and coating my insides.

"Hate to burst your bubble, Adrian," Sergei, the quietest between the three of us, enters the room smoking a cigarette. "Looks like you're going to need to keep her." He takes a seat as Ivan hands him a shot.

I lean forward for Ivan to pour me another round. "Last I checked, I don't pay you for your opinions."

Letting out a cloud of smoke into the air as he tilts his head back, Sergei smirks. "No, but my opinion saved your ass today when you almost killed her."

Prison became sort of a job recruitment, which is where most of my men are chosen. There is this unspoken camaraderie between us, having to endure the harsh circumstances and fight for survival. These are the kind of men I need to secure my place. They are my trusted enforcers.

"You just love to ruin my day."

"I told you I could get him to marry," Sergei laughs, nodding off to Ivan, who erupts into a hyena laugh.

Jokes aside, I trust Ivan and Sergei with my life. In prison, it was the three of us against everyone, prisoners and guards.

Sucking my teeth in annoyance, I sneer, "Tell me why I can't marry her, then throw her off a cliff."

"The old man was smart. He wanted to make sure his money stayed with the right person. Marrying his daughter isn't enough." Sergei drinks from his cup. "If she dies, all those assets go to the state."

Slamming the cup on the table, I yell, "Blyat."

Ivan pours me another round. "So, lock her up in a tower or in the dungeon. No one will know. There are no rules on how she lives."

"The marriage should look legitimate until the heat settles down," Sergei mentions. "Right now, it looks as though Lana has come to you as an ally for protection, thinking the killers are looking to finish what they started. If she disappears too soon, you'll get yourself locked up behind those cell bars again. This time, you know they will keep you there for good."

I sharply inhale at the inconvenience. "Is everything ready?"

"Everything is ready to go," Ivan smiles, showcasing his good tooth.

Leaving them to continue their night, I head toward the other side of the house. Living in this fortress is drastically different from my prison cell. Bearing high ceilings and a grand interior, it is the epitome of high social status, yet the irony of it being occupied by criminals makes it clear that money and power do get you far. Walking through the opulent corridors, the comparison between now and that grim prison that held me for years flickers through my mind. Sunlight from the setting sun streams through the narrow windows, casting a warm glow on the marble floors. Each step is laden with memories of those cold concrete walls, a bed of hay, and the weight of despair.

As I reach Lana's door, one of the maids is coming out. When she sees me, her face goes pale. I can tell the innocence of a person based on their reaction when I am in front of them. She is scared but remains resilient.

"Master." She bows. "I've placed the dress and shoes on the bed as you requested."

I don't want to lie and say that I don't enjoy seeing the absolute fear in someone as they stand in front of me. With endless time rotting in that hellhole, I debated whether it was better to be respected or feared. I came out of that prison fully convinced that being feared got you more respect than being kind ever did.

And I am going to make sure Lana will learn there isn't a kind bone in my body.

Chapter 2

Lana

Lost in thought, I sit on the shower floor as the water hits my body like shards of glass. Steam, thick and suffocating, clings to me like a blanket, mirroring the suffocating grief that coils in my gut. My legs, drawn tight to my chest, offer no solace against the tremor that racks my body as I gently rock myself, trying to control the volume of emotions that are suffocating me. The horrid sight of my parents cut throats on the floor as they lie in a pool of blood is something I will never forget, while the anger of the betrayal of my husband is a lesson I will always remember. You can't trust anyone.

"Lana."

The sound of my name wakes my soul before a wave of panic hits me. The door to the bathroom slides open, and in walks the man who's spared me, the man who holds my life in his cold, calculating hands. I scramble to my feet; the shower door feels like a flimsy shield against his intrusion.

"What do you want?" My voice, a choked whisper, is lost in the steam as I open the shower glass door.

The bathroom, a white-hot, steam-filled cage, distorts his form, making him seem both like a phantom and a predator. He moves toward me, a dark silhouette in the swirling vapor, radiating an unnerving calm that sends shivers crawling down my spine. The scent of his cologne, sharp and unfamiliar, wars with the metallic tang of blood still clinging to my senses. Adrian makes his way toward me as the fog molds around his body.

"Hurry up. Everyone is waiting."

"Everyone?" I question.

"It is custom to meet the family before exchanging vows, is it not?" His words are a chilling invitation, a veiled threat hanging between us.

The Sokolov family—a monstrous collection of souls—is now the last standing bratva of Moscow. It has been embedded into my head since I was a child that they were sworn enemies, and now I am at their mercy.

My throat constricts, a single, choked nod my only response. As though I am of no importance, Adrian turns around and walks out, sliding the door shut behind him, the steam curling in response and reclaiming the space. I stand under the shower, wondering how long it will take to adjust to a new home, a new life, a new...everything.

To my surprise, when I walk out of the bathroom, Adrian is standing in the bedroom, looking at his phone with his back to me. His broad shoulders seem tense. Holding the towel tightly around my body, I make my way over to the bag I quickly packed for myself, which causes him to turn around.

"Your clothes are on the bed," he nods toward the long red satin cowl neck dress.

"I'm not wearing that," I reply, opening my bag.

He moves like a viper, with a sudden, brutal strike. The bag is torn from my grasp, his fingers like steel.

"You will wear what I tell you to wear," he snarls, tossing it aside with a casual violence that sends a shudder through me. The bulging muscle in his arm is as taut as a coiled spring, speaking of the raw power he holds.

"You don't own me," I spit back.

"Once you're my wife, I will." He crosses his arms behind his back, holding his wrist in one hand. "My house, my rules. So let's get you caught up. You wear what I tell you. You will dress and undress yourself with me in the room."

"Scared I'll put a knife in my pocket?"

As he inhales, it is like watching a fire grow when adding more fuel, lifting his shirt to reveal a patchwork of scars across his abdomen and oblique muscles as though each one is a trophy—a story of survival. "I can add it to my collection," he replies with a wicked grin.

My pulse quickens as I can feel beads of sweat forming on my forehead. "You think a few cuts can scare me? You forget I grew up around men with mutations. Things far worse than what you're showing me. I was raised on stories that could make a hardened criminal weep."

"There's a big difference between hearing it and living it. You've never endured the kind of pain you saw." A dark chuckle escapes his mouth as he slowly walks toward me. "Every scar tells a story." He points to the one right above his navel. "That one there? My cellmate did this while I was asleep and recovering from another attack." He lets go of his shirt so that it covers his torso and places his arms in front of him as he holds one wrist in his hand. Adrian's mouth curves up into a smile. "I pulled the blade right out and stabbed it right into his eye, then used my bare hands to rip his other eyeball out."

He steps closer, making the tension thicken. *How can he be afraid of me when he's the one capable of taking a life?*

"I trust you just as much as you trust me."

Stopping in his tracks, he replies with a tight expression. He shoots back, "As long as you obey me, there won't be any issues. No need for trust."

There is an odd sense of a blend of challenge and connection between us in this moment, but it all disappears in the blink of an eye.

"Now get dressed," he demands.

I lift the dress off the bed to examine it. The beautiful dress is rather promiscuous for a family dinner compared to the black T-shirt and jeans he is wearing.

"It won't fit me," I toss it back onto the bed. I've only been under his roof for 3 hours. How would he know what I can fit into? I'm not the usual standard size—I come with lots of curves, and I'm no skin and bones.

"You haven't tried it on."

"I can tell—"

"Put. The. Dress. On."

I clench my fists. "I may be here because you spared my life, but I won't let you talk to me that way."

Slowly and in a calculating way, Adrian walks over to me. "You're right. I spared your life. But you're wrong if you think I can't speak to you in any way. The sooner you learn that, the better it will be for you."

"I won't let you intimidate me."

Circling around me, he stops, standing close behind me and whispers into my ear, "You don't seem like someone who is easily threatened." His nose brushes against my ear.

"But I can make your worst nightmare become a blissful dream compared to what I will do to you if you disobey."

Chapter 3

Lana

Slowly inhaling and exhaling, I speed walk behind Adrian as my feet follow like a puppy chasing him. As much as I want to mourn the loss of my family, I refuse to let him see me suffer. The way he speaks to me, the way he looks at me, I know he is going to use me as a punching bag. Any kind of weakness, he will devour it, but I know he needs me just as much as I need him.

His home, more like a castle on the inside and a fortress on the outside, is a never-ending hike, and it takes what feels like forever to finally reach the front of the house, where three cars are waiting. Leaning against one of them is one of the men from earlier today. His black silk shirt is unbuttoned, and he's wearing a gold pinky ring similar to the one Adrian wears. He holds a bottle of vodka, taking a swig, while his other arm is wrapped around a woman barely wearing clothing. She rubs his bald head and traces along the body of a snake that is tattooed on it. He is talking to another man who stands tall and lean, also wearing a silk shirt halfway unbuttoned from the top and smoking a cigarette. His hair is slicked back, tied up in a bun, with a faint beard that lines his jawline. I notice he also has the same pinky ring when the female standing beside him admires it. She's wearing enough clothing to, at least, cover the necessary parts.

"Get in the car," Adrain demands as he nods to the matte red Karlmann King SUV.

The SUV's aggressive contours cut through the dim sunlight like blades. The sleek design exudes a sense of power, with the imposing front grille and broad stance commanding attention. As the sunset casts a warm glow, the matte finish absorbs the light, giving it an almost other-worldly presence.

Adrian's sharp features are illuminated by the faint glow of the vehicle's LED lights, revealing a confident yet dangerous aura as he heads toward the group. Wearing a fitted black leather jacket, Adrian glances around, his piercing eyes scanning the surroundings with intensity. The SUV's imposing silhouette looms behind him, a perfect reflection of its owner—bold, unyielding, and ready to strike at a moment's notice.

Doing as I am told, I can't take my eyes off them conversing. I've been around scary men my whole life, but I know they don't compare. There is no humanity left inside of them, and yet they are alluring. As Adrian heads back toward the car, I look forward and pull down the mirror to check my hair, which is pulled back in a sleek ponytail as a distraction from struggling to push down my insecurities. Looking back at my face, I can't help but critically assess my reflection. My confidence is an illusion; I look nothing like those two women whose only curves are their breasts. I flip the mirror back up once the driver's door opens, letting in a refreshing breeze that seems to break me from my pity party.

The ride is mostly silent until I break it with a question. "When can I properly bury my family?"

"You have no family."

"Because you took them from me," I snap.

I feel my head forcefully pulled back, and a fist grips my ponytail. "The quicker you forget them, the easier it will be to move on."

Holding the steering wheel with his other hand, he drives faster.

"Let go of me." Struggling to get out of his grip, I know it is useless.

"You don't get to tell me what to do," he sneers as he pulls over.

Unbuckling his seatbelt and then mine, he gets out of the car, still holding onto my ponytail, dragging me out with him through the driver's side. Stumbling out of the car, my feet find the ground. Adrian throws me up against the car and gets in my face.

"If you even mention your family, you won't see them buried at all." His mouth brushes against my ear. "Understood."

"Yes," I hold back from crying.

My body shakes involuntarily, and the more I try to make it stop, the more I shake. The cool metal of the car presses against my back as Adrian steps closer, his intense gaze locking onto mine with an almost predatory focus. The street is dimly lit, shadows coiling around us like a living thing, but all I can see is him—his jaw clenched, and eyes sharp enough to cut glass.

"Stop shaking," he commands, his voice low and gravelly, sending an uncomfortable thrill down my spine.

"I'm trying," I reply as I look down.

His hands grip my arms in an attempt to hold me steady. I brace myself. He is looking to scare me into submission, but he has no idea that I'm not new to this treatment.

"Look at me," he demands.

My heart races, pounding hard enough to escape the prison of my ribcage. I feel the heat radiating from his body, a stark contrast to the chilly night air. He leans in, pinning me not just against the car but with his presence, an invisible weight breathing urgency into the moment. His hands grip my arms tighter with intentional pressure, forcing me to meet his searing gaze.

When my eyes meet his, I can barely manage to catch my breath. He is a storm wrapped in flesh and blood, fierce and unpredictable, and here I am, caught in his eye, trembling like a leaf in the wind. His gray eyes are captivating but hold nothing behind them. With each second that ticks by, the distance between terror and fascination blurs, leaving me breathless in a way I can't quite understand.

He lets me go and steps back. When he raises his hand to comb back his hair, I flinch. It's a natural reaction, but I am embarrassed that he notices. He doesn't need confirmation; he seems to know the reason why I have that reaction. For a moment, I think I see some kind of sympathy on his face, but with a blink of an eye, it is gone, and he gets back into the car.

Chapter 4

Adrian

Driving in dead silence, I put all the weight of my feet on the gas pedal. Lana sits nestled close to the window without saying a word. The look on her face when she flinched replays in my mind. Maybe it's a good thing she can be so easily frightened; it will make having her around easier to manage. Making a sharp turn into the driveway, I wave to the guard to let him know it's me without having to stop. Men are lined along the property line with guns, standing at attention, waiting for an enemy to strike at any given moment. It was unlike Lana's family, whose home was barely a challenge to enter.

As I park in my designated spot, I figure giving Lana a quick pep talk will be helpful.

"Everyone at the table will despise you." I shift the car into park. "Don't take it personally."

She scoffs. "Doesn't get as personal as earlier today." She turns her head to face me but is looking down.

"You look at me when you speak."

Her eyes lift to meet mine. I am wrong. She is holding back, and I can't help but smirk. "If you have the urge to hit me, go ahead." It's a dare that I know she won't take.

She lifts her hand and slaps me right in the face. Some set of balls. I admire her pushback, dancing along the line without crossing it. She waited for permission to act and then didn't hold back. The bold and unwise act makes my cock twitch. I grab her round face, gripping her jaw tightly.

"Someone likes it rough," I mock.

A tear slips down her cheek. It's a sad victory, but a victory nonetheless. Letting go of her chin, I grab her hair and pull out the hair tie, letting her golden-brown hair cascade around her. I laugh as she looks at me with utter fear.

"Hair stays down, unless I say otherwise."

Those big brown eyes are staring at me while her jaw drops in shock. Using my knuckle, I lift her chin so that her mouth closes. Her soft skin against my knuckle feels like a pillow, giving me an odd sense of comfort, which makes me uncomfortable. Quickly cutting contact, I get out of the car and sharply inhale the cool air. The evening air feels thick with anticipation. No one has any idea what to expect tonight.

Lana steps out of the car and adjusts her dress. Her curves are a celebration of femininity. Every voluptuous line tells a story of allure. The red satin fabric seems to be made for her. The way her hips sway lightly. She turns in a smooth rhythm that seems to hold a spell over me at first, before shaking my head from the intrusive thoughts. The loosely fitted dress hugs her perfectly, accentuating her waist and flattering the soft swell of her thighs, whispering secrets of sensuality. *She's an enemy*, I recite in my mind.

The house manager opens the door before I get to knock.

"Ah, master Adrian. Your family has been waiting for some time."

"I waited 5 years to come home, they can wait a few hours for me."

I guide Lana into the house. As we step into the grand foyer of my family's mansion, the familiar mix of pride and resentment twist in my stomach. The towering columns and extravagant decor always feel like a constant reminder of the legacy I am bound to. The sheer opulence of the place masks a lineage steeped in brutality, and every corner of this house whispers of the crimes we have committed for power. The hall is decorated with the crests of families we have taken down, with an open spot made for the Petrovi.

As we enter the dining room, the atmosphere thickens, draped in the oppressive weight of familial scrutiny. The long mahogany table is a stage for the pretense that defines our lives—confirmation of my family's wealth and standing. Lana's nervous energy radiates from her as we approach the table, and I can sense her discomfort. She will need to get used to this.

At the head of the table sits my father, drinking from his chalice cup made of pure gold. My mother sits to his right, dolled up as usual, never a hair out of place. Beside her is my sister, Bianca, a spitting image of my mother. Across from them sits my younger brother Gil, who is a mix of both my parents—blonde hair from my mother and the same facial structure as my father.

Gil chokes up a laugh. "Adrian, this may be by far the craziest shit you have pulled yet."

My father gets to his feet. "Why is there a Petrova in my home and not at the morgue?"

"Now is that how you speak to your future daughter-in-law?" I comment as I pull out a seat for Lana on the other side of the table.

I've earned my keep and sit at the other head of the table beside Lana. My father wouldn't be the most powerful crime lord in Moscow if it weren't for me eliminating everyone else.

"Don't be ridiculous, Adrian." My father's tone is stern. "I sent you to kill them all, not keep one as a souvenir."

"Lana and I have fallen in love." The words leave my mouth as an attempt not to laugh. "We have come to an agreement."

I am met with blank stares. From my peripheral view, Lana is the most shocked.

Watching my father's anger building up, my mother swoops in. "Boris, dear. Our son has suffered for years. If he says he's in love, why not let him enjoy it?"

"Olga, you truly believe this Petrova is worthy?" my father replies.

"There are plenty of eligible women in this city who would have been a better fit for him." My mother's voice is a polished blade, warm yet cutting as she rakes her gaze over Lana, noting every detail. "But this is who he has chosen."

"When should we begin planning the wedding?" my father asks as he snaps his fingers for another drink.

"Two days."

"Two days?!" Bianca blurts out. "Adrian, this is outrageous." She nearly snarls at Lana, who remains silent beside me.

"No bachelor party?" Gil asks with a shake of his head.

"I think you overdid it for my welcome home celebration."

Gil knows how to throw a party bender with the hottest

females, and he did not disappoint in welcoming me back home after getting out of prison. A dish is placed in front of me with three Pelmeni neatly positioned on a bed of fresh dill, with dill oil drizzled on top, and melted butter in a separate dish for dipping.

"Thank you," Lana smiles at the man who serves her.

No one else at the table thanks the server. We never thank anyone for something we expect to be done. The servers work for money—why would they need a thank you? I'm not the only one who notices. Casually tipping over the glass of wine in front of me, I watch Lana as she sees it spill everywhere, and a crowd of servants comes to quickly clean it up and pour me a new glass as I sit and don't say a word.

Lana seems to have understood my message.

Chapter 5

Lana

Their eyes, cold chips of glacial ice, bore into me. If looks can kill, this family won't just use it—they will weaponize it. The air hangs thick, a suffocating cloud of unspoken threats, chilling me to the bone more than the polished marble floor beneath my feet. The scent of lilies placed on the table, usually sweet, feels cloying, a sickly perfume masking the stench of their predatory intent. They are vultures dressed in designer clothing and masked by impeccable manners, but they are heartless. Adrian made it clear that they didn't converse with the help in the house. *Message received.*

There is a sudden shift in the room. The icy air seems to crackle with a sudden, dangerous heat. A woman enters with long, raven hair cascading down her back, framing a face that is both breathtaking and exotic. Her body, a masterpiece, as it moves with grace against the tight black dress she wears, showcasing her long legs. Her plump lips curve into a smile that seems sweet and genuine. "Sorry, everyone, my appointment ran late."

Gil's hand is possessive on the curve of her spine. "Did you have a good session?"

Her voice, a silken whisper that can shatter glass, replies, "Always." The kiss that followed is an affectionate display of a loving couple.

"Raya, meet Adrian's bride-to-be, Lana." The words hang in the air, heavy with malice.

Raya's gaze locks onto mine, making me lose my breath when she looks in my direction. "Bride?" she echoes, looking at me and then Adrian. "Congratulations," she smiles as she approaches me. "I'm Raya, Gil's wife."

She pulls me into a hug, which takes me off guard. She then turns to Adrian and gives him a big embrace.

"Wedding is day after tomorrow," Gil states. "My brother won't even give me time to throw him a proper bachelor party."

Raya gives a soft laugh as though she wouldn't expect anything else. "Oh, that's quick. Should I help with planning?"

Their mother, a woman whose face is a roadmap of cruelty etched by years of ruthless ambition, cuts in, her voice a sharp crack of ice. "Nonsense, I'll have everything planned. Everyone just needs to show up."

A server comes to collect my plate and replace it with another. Herring, carrots, beets, and potatoes—a carefully crafted tower that mocks my hollow stomach. Beside it is braised cabbage, crowned with a careless extravagance of red caviar. Each dish is a masterpiece of culinary artistry.

I force a smile to the impassive server, whose eyes hold the same chilling emptiness as all the Sokolovs have. It feels odd not showing some kind of appreciation.

"Is that enough for you?" Their mother's voice, like a viper's strike, cuts through the forced civility. "I'm sure you're used to larger portions."

Instantly, I feel my cheeks flush as I hold back from breaking down. My vision becomes blurry as I do my best not to blink.

"I'm sure Adrian's chef can whip you up something when you get back."

No one moves or makes a sound. I have learned to handle my mother's remarks on my weight, even when she did it publicly, but it always hurt the same.

"Better to have a well-fed wife than one who throws it up afterward." Adrian picks up his fork and takes a bite of his food.

I am taken aback. No one ever stands up for me—not my father, not my husband. The room remains quiet for a few minutes before the family carries on with conversation as I sit silently. I can feel the weight of everyone's sharp and scrutinizing gaze as I lift the fork that holds a tiny piece of herring to my mouth and chew as slowly as possible. The fork feels heavy from the suffocating pressure to appear composed and invisible in my own insecurities. Carefully observing everyone at the table, no one finishes their dish, so I do the same.

"Do you like Medovik, Lana?" Raya asks me. "The chef here makes the best."

A server comes to remove my plate and replaces it with a slice of honey cake. My eyes begin to swell with the memory of the last time I had some.

"My mother loved it," I reply in a soft tone. "I'm not one for sweets."

"I wouldn't have guessed that," their mother comments

nonchalantly. "Adrian always requested a piece after dinner. It's his favorite."

Adrian picks up the piece of his cake with his bare hand and takes a bite. "I've lost the taste for it." Throwing it back onto the plate, he gets to his feet and looks down at me. "Get to the car."

Quickly getting to my feet, I follow behind one of the housemaids, who takes me to the front door. She practically kicks me out, shutting the door behind me once I step outside. The car is locked, so I stand there shivering until what feels like an eternity, when Adrian strides toward me with a storm of rage swirling deep in his gray eyes. His jaw is clenched, and his brows are knitted tightly together. Something is wrong—very wrong. It appears as though he is ready to walk through me as his hard body collides into mine, pinning me against the car. The palms of my hands are pushed against his hard chest, trying to create some kind of push back, but I'm not strong enough.

"Open your mouth," he barks at me.

"What?" I reply, looking at him with fear and confusion, which is then replaced with shock when he shoves a piece of Medovik into my mouth.

Adrian forces the cake into my mouth—the sweetness floods my senses as I attempt not to choke. The taste of honey clashes with the tension crackling in the air as I look into his eyes. They are fierce, battling something beneath the surface, but they soften for a fleeting moment when I begin to gag. Pulling himself away from me, he takes the remainder of the cake held in his hand and throws it as far as he can while I fall to my knees onto the pavement beside the car. Spitting out what remains in my mouth while gasping for air, each breath a struggle against the wave of panic washing over me. The coolness of the pavement somehow grounds me as I steady my racing heart.

"Get up!" Adrian shouts at me, his jaw tightening in a struggle of emotions.

Managing to get to my feet, I spit right onto his face. Taking the back of his hand, he wipes it off as though he is victorious. "Let's see how long before you despise me."

Shaking, I spit out, "Will that feed your ego?" Wiping the crumbs on my face. "Don't count on me to do that."

"You're a porcelain doll, and I intend to smash you into pieces," he growls. "I'll make you suffer each day I allow you to live."

"Give me your best shot," I challenge.

The smirk on his face is sinister yet somehow alluring, sending chills through my body. I watch him walk to the driver's side and get inside the car. Taking a deep breath, I open the passenger door, still in shock. Before getting in, I look back at the house to see his family watching out the window.

Chapter 6

Adrian

"Send her to her room," I demand of a house servant as we walk through the door.

Lana refuses to look at me, and the fact that I don't care how she feels makes it easier to go about the night. Without looking behind me, I head toward the billiard room where Ivan and Sergei are indulging in their women of the night. Once I come into view, Sergei shoots Ivan a look.

"Okay, ladies." Ivan throws his woman off him. "Time to call it a night."

"Already?" one of them drunkenly slurs.

"It's not an option," Ivan's voice threatens them as he pulls out his gun.

The women know better than to say anything else, and off they run. Sitting on the edge of the sofa, I bend down and sniff a line of coke off the table.

"Someone is on edge," Sergei comments as he lights up a cigarette. "I take it dinner didn't go well."

"It went fine," I reply.

"Nothing with your father is fine," Ivan eggs on as he places his gun on the table.

Taking the nearest bottle of vodka, I take a chug. "My father has a final request before stepping down."

"What more could he want?" Sergei asks. "You went to prison for him. You got out and eliminated any competition in this city."

"He wants me to make an alliance with Dmitri Vaskov."

"For what?" Sergei questions. "You don't need any more alliances. I don't see how Vladimir would be any more useful than we would need him to be."

"Lana's father and Vladimir were battling over territorial grounds in Lefortovo District."

Ivan seems to shrug it off as he snorts another line of cocaine. "We have the manpower, so I'm not concerned."

"My father seems to be." I do another line of coke.

Sergei puts out his cigarette in his ashtray with more force than needed.

"Something on your mind?" I question him.

He is hesitant at first but eventually caves. "Your father doesn't need to run the show anymore. You've earned your keep ten times over. You should break ties and run your own show. Why wait for him to hand over his reign?"

"I want him to bow out with grace. If he doesn't, then we can handle it from there," I assure him.

Sergei doesn't seem convinced. "Okay."

I get to my feet. "Now let's go solidify my place as Russia's King of Criminals."

* * *

The air hangs thick with the scent of stale beer, cheap vodka, and desperation. We move through the dimly lit backroom of the Golden Fleece, a bar notorious for its clientele and the even more notorious things that happen within its shadowed corners. It isn't a place for social gathering; it is a battlefield of subtle gestures, whispered words, and unspoken threats.

My eyes, sharp and calculating, scan the room. Familiar faces—some etched with the lines of age and hardship, others bearing the youthful arrogance of newly arrived players—acknowledge my presence with nods, averted glances, or the chilling absence of any reaction at all.

"He's right there," Ivan whispers into my ear and nods in the direction of Dmitri Vaskov.

In a cornered booth, Dmitri sits, a hulking brute with a reputation for sadistic cruelty, leaning against a crumbling wall, his gaze lingering on me with a mixture of uncertainty and apprehension. Although I have never had issues with him in the past, he sends a silent war of glares in our direction. Meeting his gaze unflinchingly, offering no concessions, I make my way to his table and sit across from him. The conversation won't be about friendship; it will be about power. It's about creating a balance between the threat of force and the allure of mutual benefit.

"You survived the Black Dolphin?" Dmitri holds up his beverage in salute.

"Did you expect otherwise?" I reply almost in a joking tone.

"No one survives that place."

"I'm not just anyone."

With a sharp inhale, he releases his breath slowly. "I know why you're here."

"Good. It saves me from explanation. How can we settle this amicably?"

"Settle it?" Dmitri challenges. "There is no settling. I'll go to war if needed."

"Why don't we avoid bloodshed over some land that will cost us both men?"

"Some land?" he mocks. "It holds prime real estate. It's the perfect location for the midway transport of products. That was key to the Petrovi powerhouse. So, I don't mind losing a few men for the time being."

"We can both utilize the warehouse located there."

A sarcastic grin crosses his face while shaking his head. "You and I have lots in common. One being we don't share. So I don't see that lasting long."

"Fair enough. What if I wager a valuable asset of mine?"

"And what, Adrian, is your generous offer to stem this tide of blood?"

"My sister, Bianca. Her hand in marriage. She'll bring influence that will outweigh having that territory."

"Influence? Or do you mean leverage? You're proposing a union built on...pragmatism, not affection."

"Are we not pragmatic men?"

He takes a moment to think it over. "What guarantees do I have that this isn't some ploy to undermine me?"

"This is not a ploy. This is securing peace."

"Peace, you say. A fragile thing," Dimitri says, arching an eyebrow as if he's contemplating the weight of the universe.

"Consider the alternative, Dmitri. Endless bloodshed. A war neither of us wants to deal with. Marriage to my sister comes with the promise that you keep your life." I emphasize, leaning in as if we're exchanging recipes rather than threats.

"They say you are heartless. Treating everything like a business transaction, nothing more, nothing less."

"You marry Bianca, I take the territory, and you may use it to cross your products safely into Kazakhstan. What's the harm in playing matchmaker?" I grin, my charm dripping like honey.

"No. I do not accept your terms." He lifts his glass to his mouth for a sip.

In a swift, dramatic gesture, I snatch his glass from his hand and slam it onto the edge of the table, creating a jagged edge. The glass shatters like my hopes for a diplomatic evening, sending shimmering shards flying. "I don't accept your rejection." With another swift move, I slice his face.

His men spring forward, concern painted across their faces like they're watching a horror flick, but Ivan and Sergei are quicker, pulling their guns with poise, shots ringing out before the men can react.

Dmitri falls to his knees, clutching his face that's gushing with blood. "I'll never agree!" he shouts, knowing where his fate lies.

"That's unfortunate to hear," I reply with a mockingly sympathetic tone as I pull out my PB pistol.

While aiming at his forehead, he mutters a prayer. I give him the courtesy to finish before I pull the trigger.

"Well, that settles that," Ivan says, placing his gun away.

"That was surprisingly easy," Sergei smirks. "How about a round of cards?"

Chapter 7

Lana

I barely sleep through the night, as visions of my parents vividly replay in my mind. I bolt upright, gasping for breath, the weight of dread pressing down on me. Flashbacks of my family flood my thoughts, weighing heavily on me. Sitting up in bed, my body is moist from the sweat of fear, awoken by a dream of shadows twisted into monstrous forms that held me captive as I ran down a dark hallway that seemed to stretch endlessly. Looking at the clock, it reads 2:37 am. In the dead of night, darkness cloaks the room with an eerier stillness. The room is bare, only having a bed, a nightstand, and a dresser. The walls are plain, and the floor is concrete. A fleeting thought cuts through the haze of panic; there isn't a shot in hell I'll survive. Maybe I can make a run for it.

Throwing off the covers, my pulse quickens as my senses heighten. Quickly jumping out of bed, I make my way toward the only window in the room. The moon hangs high in the sky, casting a silvery glow that lights up the ground below. I lift the latch and slowly pull the window open. The cool breeze caresses my skin as I peer out into the night, measuring the distance to the ground. The soft grass below promises a landing that won't break my bones. I hesitate for a moment, my instincts screaming that the danger lies not in the leap but rather in remaining within these walls. This is my only chance.

I make my way back to the bed and strip it of all the covers. Tying them together, I form a rope and throw one end out the window, then tie the other to the metal bed frame. Summoning all the courage I can muster, I climb over the sill and swing my legs out and around the sheets. Slowly, I secure myself on the sheets and begin to descend, praying with all my being that I don't fall or that the sheets don't rip. When my feet hit the ground with a silent thud, I take a deep breath as adrenaline surges through my veins. Without hesitation or looking back, I run. Unsure where I am heading, my feet eventually hit solid ground. I glance over my shoulder as I continue to bolt into the surrounding darkness, making sure no one can see me.

But within a couple of steps, I come to a screeching halt when beams of light head my way. I am in the driveway, and I can hear the engines of cars speeding toward me, causing me to turn around and run in the direction I have just come from. It isn't long before the cars catch up and circle me. Three vehicles' headlights are on me, and I'm trapped. I fall to my knees, trying to catch my breath, when I hear three car doors shut.

"Lana," a low voice breaks through the night air, sending shivers cascading down my spine.

His footsteps become louder as he approaches me. Kneeling down on one leg, he takes my face, forcing me to look at him. "I thought we had an agreement," he teases, but the undercurrent of menace in his tone sends tremors through my body. "You're getting cold feet now?"

"I can't do this," I breathe as I shake in fear.

"Which part?"

"All of it."

He lets go of my face and stands up. I am barely able to see with the headlights so bright in my eyes. I hear something hit the ground, and when I look down, it's a gun.

"Go ahead then," he insists. "Take me out. There's enough in there to get me, Ivan, and Sergei...as long as you have good aim."

My mouth goes dry. I grab the gun and quickly get to my feet, holding it out toward him. There is no fear in his eyes, which terrifies me.

"Do you think I won't actually pull the trigger?" My voice is blended with defiance and fierce conviction as I grip the handle of the gun.

"I guess we will find out." He maintains his causal demeanor.

I pull the trigger, but no bullet comes out.

Shit.

Chapter 8

Adrian

She pulled the trigger. The resounding snap echoes through the night air. A blank shot reverberates, ringing with a hollow sound that fills the stillness of the moment. The force jolts against her hand, and a gleam of surprise dances across her face. Something in her isn't afraid of me, and I'm impressed by her stupid bravery. Did she really believe she could take three criminals out on her own? Did she really believe that I would hand her a loaded gun?

"Are you done now?" I ask, mocking this moment.

She throws the gun toward me in surrender. Walking toward her, I lift her over my shoulder and walk her into the house. I don't stop until we are in my room, where I lock us inside. She doesn't scream or say a word—she must be terrified of the unknown. Practically dropping her on the ground at the end of my bed, I pull out a key from under my mattress. I watch her face as she realizes the end of the bed is a pillory. The ledge is painted all black, so you won't notice it unless you're paying attention. The three holes are big enough for securing a neck and hands.

I unlock the lock and lift the top portion. "Get in."

Lana steps back. "This isn't the 1800s. I'm not a prisoner for you to display."

Little does she know that once we are married, she practically will be. "Afraid I'll keep you here until the wedding day?"

"I wouldn't put it past you."

"You tried to run. You thought you could escape me, but you were wrong," my deep voice rumbles, my tone calm yet commanding. I stand before her, my tall frame casting a shadow over her figure. "Now, you must face the consequences of your actions."

Lana's eyes dart to the pillory, and her throat seems to constrict at the sight of it. "I...I'm sorry," she murmurs, her voice barely above a whisper. "I didn't think—"

"You didn't think," I interrupt, my words sharp yet measured. "That's the problem, isn't it? You act without considering the consequences."

I reach out, my large hand grasping her chin firmly, tilting her face up to meet my gaze. My touch is gentle yet unyielding, a reminder of my control. "You belong to me, Lana."

"Who's to say you're good enough for that privilege?" she shoots back.

Her breathing is heavy as her breasts rise and fall with her nipples poking out. She is dressed in a simple white shift nightdress, its fabric thin enough to reveal the curves of her body. Her hair cascades over her shoulders, framing her face. Her bare feet are planted firmly on the cold ground, almost in confident defiance, but her face tells a different story, a mix of fear and something else—something she refuses to acknowledge. It is as though my dominance has a way of unraveling her, of making her question her own desires. Walking toward her, I get close enough to make her breathing increase, almost panting.

Lana's cheeks flush, a clear sign her body is betraying her as a tingle of excitement courses, and noticeable goosebumps rise along her smooth skin. I can tell by the way her nipples tighten under the thin fabric of her nightdress that although she wants to push me away, her body has other ideas.

"Get in there."

"No," she replies.

"I guess you prefer learning things the hard way."

Grabbing her by the hair, I shove her onto the bed and toward the pillory, forcing her head down so that her neck fits into the space along with her wrists in their proper place, slamming it shut and quickly locking it. The air in the dimly lit room mixes with the scent of leather and polished wood, mingling with the faint tang of sweat. My eyes fix on Lana with an intensity as I watch her trapped in the pillory, supporting her body on the mattress by propping herself onto her knees. She had tried to run, foolishly believing she could escape my grasp, but now here she is, bound and helpless, her wrists restrained by soft leather cuffs attached to a sturdy wooden frame.

The pillory is a favorite of mine, but I'm not looking to pleasure Lana at all, despite how beautiful this sight is. Standing at the opposite end of the bed where Lana's head pokes out, my eyes darken with satisfaction at the terrified look on her face. Her breath quickens as she realizes there is no escape from the wooden beams pressing against her arms, holding her firmly in place as my piercing gaze locks onto hers. Lana is at my mercy. Her chest rises and falls with each shallow breath, and my cock begins to harden, feeding off her discomfort mixed with this sense of desire radiating off her.

As I stand in front of her, I reach out and trace a finger along her jawline, my touch both gentle and possessive. "You're going to watch me, Lana," I say with a firm voice. "And if you look away, I will rip your eyeballs out."

She watches as I take a step back. With deliberate slowness, I begin to unbuckle my belt, the sound of metal against leather echoing in the quiet room. Lana's cheeks flush a faint pink, spreading across her pale skin as she watches me pull out my thick, heavy cock from my pants.

After spitting into my hand, I begin stroking myself slowly, my movements deliberate and teasing. Lana's eyes are glued to me, her body responding despite her attempts to resist. I watch as her thighs press together as though suppressing her arousal. Am I dealing with a little vixen?

"You're enjoying this, aren't you?" I tease, my voice dripping with satisfaction as my strokes quicken.

Lana's eyes widen, her cheeks darkening further. "You could only wish."

She wants to deny it, to pretend she isn't affected, but her body gives her away. Reveling in the torture, I jerk myself faster. With a final, intense stroke, I groan, my body tensing as I reach my climax. Her breath catches in her throat as I step closer, positioning myself directly in front of her. Lana watches, transfixed, as my cum shoots through the air in thick, hot streams across her face. Lana's eyes widen as she feels it drip down her forehead and cheeks, cum filling her nostrils and glistening on her face.

"Don't pull shit like that again," I demand. "Or I will have every one of my men do this and whatever else they want to you and leave you locked up in this pillory until you die."

She looks at me with full rage that almost makes me hard again. There is this fierceness in her eyes that tells me she doesn't care, so I need extra assurance she won't run away again. Pulling my pants back up, I pull out my phone and snap a photo of Lana in the pillory with my cum dripping down her face.

"For me later," I wink at her.

The look of defeat finally crosses her face. If I ever leaked this photograph, no man would take her seriously, and she would be labeled a whore. Reputation in the bratva is everything, but the women have it the roughest. It is okay to be a whore in private but not for everyone to see.

"I get it," she surrenders. "I won't run. Now get me out of here."

Letting out a chuckle. "You seem to like it in there."

"Adrian. Get me out."

"Beg me."

Frustrated, she shakes her head. "Your ego is bigger than your ability to be empathetic."

"You really shouldn't deny me," I warn.

"You really shouldn't underestimate me," Lana spits back.

"Says the person trapped in a pillory."

"Then leave me here. I will never beg you to spare me."

"I bet I can get you to."

With both hands, Lana gives me the middle finger. The restraints around her wrists clank at the gesture.

"Is that your way of challenging me?" I smirk.

"There's no way in hell you can make me do anything. I don't care how badly you torture me."

"Let's find out."

Using one hand, I wipe as much of my cum off her face as possible. Walking over to the mattress, I hike one knee onto the bed and lift her dress up so that her ass is exposed. I place my other knee on her lower leg and my free hand on her ankle, pinning them down so she won't move. Her panties are damp, her clit clearly aching for attention. This is going to be too easy. Using my teeth, I rip off the thin lace. Taking the cum in my hand, I lather her up from her pussy to the top of the crack of her ass. Her body immediately tenses as she remains positioned on her knees. I begin to rub her firmly from her clit to the top of her ass crack to stimulate her as much as possible. One time, two times, three times, then *SLAP*. The sound of my hand hitting her pussy echoes in the room. Lana gasps and tries to move, but between me and the pillory holding her down, it makes it impossible. I glide my hand again from top to bottom; one time, two times, three times, then *SLAP*. This time, Lana lets out a moan. I repeat this motion over and over, each time my slap getting harder and more intense against her pussy and ass crack. Lana begins to arch her back, and I am certain she is thrusting her hips against my hand.

"Let me hear you beg, Lana," my voice husky as I try to suppress my own desire to plunge my cock inside of her.

"F-f-fuck. You," she lets out in a breath.

"You're soaked. And I won't stop until you beg me."

Gliding my hand again from top to bottom, one time, two times, three times, then *SLAP*. Then *SLAP* again. Then again. My cock is rock solid, listening to the slaps, her moaning and screaming in pleasure. I am going to make her beg one way or another. I know I hit the sweet spot when she freezes with her back arching and hips thrusting forward with a large gasp. She's at the edge now, and I bring the force up to a ten. Screams of pleasure erupt from her mouth, her pussy contracting hard.

"Beg for it," I whisper, my voice low and teasing as I quicken the rhythm, savoring the way her breath hitches.

My fingers glisten with her juices, a testament to my dominance.

"Please," she breathes out, her desperation palpable.

"Please, what?" I taunt, watching her writhe beneath my command, helpless and beautiful.

"I don't know," she moans, lost in the haze of ecstasy. "Just please!! Bozhe moy, I need it!"

Hearing her call out *my god* in a way as though she is calling out my name almost has me busting all over the sheets. It gives me just as much satisfaction as sexually torturing her.

"You're begging for it now, aren't you?"

"Yes. Yes. Yes." Her voice is a symphony of longing, and I relish in her surrender.

Lana's body suddenly collapses fully onto the bed, shutting her legs closed with an orgasm that erupts through her body and out of her mouth. I remove myself from her to just watch. When she finally settles down, I walk around the bed to see her face flushed red and sweaty, with her eyes fully dilated.

"Was that so hard?" I smirk and then turn to walk away.

"You're not going to let me out?" she voices breathlessly.

Turning around to face her, I tease, "Why would I do that?"

"You said you would if I begged."

"No," I correct her, "I said I bet I can make you beg. I never agreed to let you go."

Lana's jaw drops, and she goes pale.

"Have a good night," I wink and walk out of the room.

Chapter 9

Lana

My eyes flutter open to the harsh light of morning filtering through the tiny window of the room. Confusion clouds my thoughts until I register the stinging ache in my neck and the unyielding grip of the pillory holding me in place. Panic bubbles up in my chest as memories from the previous night rush back—my desperate attempt to escape, prevented by the very man who now stands before me. I thought it was a dream, but this cruelty is my reality.

"You made yourself comfortable." Adrian's voice drips with mock enthusiasm as he leans against the doorframe, arms crossed with a cup of water in one hand, amusement dancing in his eyes. "Did you sleep well?"

"What kind of monster locks someone up like this?" I shoot back, straining against the restraints.

"A monster who doesn't take kindly to ungrateful cunts trying to run away. You think I'm just going to let you waltz out after sparing your life?" His tone turns icy, matching the glint of malice in his eyes.

"It was worth a try," I snap, my voice filled with defiance. "You think this is going to teach me a lesson?"

"Maybe it will teach you to think twice before plotting your next escape," he replies, stepping forward to loom over me, his body only inches from my face. "Next time I won't be so kind."

I glare at him, my pulse quickening with anger. "Maybe if you treated me with some respect instead of like a prisoner, I wouldn't feel the need to escape!"

A smirk curls his lips. "Respect? And what would that look like?"

He makes it sound as though the word *respect* is a foreign term.

With determination, I retort, "You think you can control me by locking me up in this contraption?"

"Control? Oh please, Lana. It's not about control; it's about discipline. Loyalty." He leans in closer, his breath hot against my cheek. "And if you think you can talk your way out of this, you're mistaken."

I take a deep breath, my frustration boiling beneath the surface. "Look, I won't run away again. Just...let me out of this thing."

"Please?" he echoes mockingly, raising an eyebrow. "Or do I need to make you beg for it again?"

"If you ever do that again, I'll take my own life."

"Do what exactly?" he squats in front of me so we are eye to eye. His gray eyes seem lighter today but still hold this unsettling feeling. "The part where I turned your pussy beet red or when I made you cum so hard you called me your god."

Doing my best to control my boiling rage, I hang my head low to compose myself with a few breaths and then look back up to face him. "I have to pee."

Adrian studies me for a long moment, his expression shifting from amusement to contemplation. "My family is here for breakfast. You need to be on your best behavior."

I let out a laugh. "Not much I can do locked in here."

He extends his arm that holds the glass of water toward me. My mouth is dry, but I would rather pass out than take a sip.

"Drink." He forces the water into my mouth, but I spit it out all over him.

He growls in frustration but refrains from lashing out.

With a smirk on my face, I say, "You can keep me here. I'll be just fine."

He stands up, and I am waiting for whatever I have coming to me. To my surprise, I feel the top of the pillory lift, allowing me to lift my head and sit up on my knees on the mattress. My hands, however, are still restrained.

"We need to make them believe we are in love," Adrian said.

"Them?" I question.

"My family. Everyone. This has to look legitimate."

"Why? Once we are married, it won't matter. What's to say you won't lock me in this forever?"

Adrian shifts on his feet. Clearly, he isn't used to anyone questioning his commands. As he reaches to release my hands, he seems skeptical whether to trust me.

"Play the part, and I give you my word I won't put you back in here."

"Even if I try to escape again?" I arch my brow, testing the limit.

He growls again. "Lana."

"Fine," I huff.

I'm not exactly sure what a loving marriage is. My father berated my mother, and my husband barely acknowledged me. If playing pretend is going to make this easier and guarantee my protection, then so be it.

Chapter 10

Adrian

Lana is making my blood pressure go through the roof. I can't trust her to behave, but I need to show her some compassion in hopes she will act accordingly. I hand her the cup of water, which I expected her to throw in my face, but instead, she takes it from me and drinks from it. I can tell she wants to resist it, but her dry lips are begging for hydration. Watching her gulp the entire cup of water with drops sliding down her neck, I can't help but think back to last night, listening to her moaning. Having full control of her was different than having full control over anyone else—it was exhilarating.

Handing me the empty cup, Lana asks, "Why is it so important that your family believes this is real?"

"You're a good distraction. They will hate you for being a Petrova but keep you alive because that will be the only thing that will make them believe I still have humanity left in me. People walk around me like they are standing on sharp blades, afraid that if they aren't careful enough, I will slice through them. A bratva leader can't easily lose control when there is so much on the line."

"So keeping me alive because of my inheritance has nothing to do with it?" she shoots back.

"Of course it does, but they don't need to know specifics. That will be just more people to add to the list of 'who to watch out for.'"

"Okay," she nods.

"Come here." I step close to the bed.

Lana makes her way to the edge of the mattress on her knees. Grabbing the fabric of her dress, I pull her into me, my hands holding her waist as my mouth is in the crook of her neck.

"What are you doing?" She tries to push me away but isn't strong enough.

"Making it look like we had a good night," I reply.

I sink my teeth into her skin and begin sucking on her neck.

"Ouch!" Lana tries to push me away. "You're hurting me!"

After a moment, I release her skin from my mouth but move it further up, creating a trail. I hold her against me as she continues to push me away, except I get carried away. I haven't even realized I am now lying on top of her, pinning her arms over her head and rocking my hips against her in between her legs as I devour her neck to the point of Lana panting. I can't stop—I don't want to, and Lana doesn't either. I pull up her dress as she unbuttons my pants, both eager for a pounding, but before I can slam my cock inside of her, there's a knock at the door.

"Not now!" I shout.

Ivan drums on the door once more. "Adrian, it's important."

Ivan wouldn't ever interrupt a fucking unless it was important, and it snaps me back into place. Quickly removing myself from a breathless half naked Lana, I adjust myself and walk away, shaking off the erection. Exiting the room, Ivan and a head guard for one of my warehouses are standing there.

"There's a problem."

"What kind of problem?" my tone agitated.

"Shipment is being stalled at the warehouse."

"By what?"

"He claims to be family."

"Let's head out," I reply. "Give me a second." I briefly walk back into the room. "I'll be back later.

* * *

We are in a van with blackout windows just outside the city limits to meet whatever disruption is being done to block my shipment. Ivan arranges an impromptu meeting with this anonymous person at an abandoned warehouse. Upon arrival, my men are unsure whether there are enough of them surrounding the property should something go wrong.

Ivan and Sergei enter the warehouse with me. In the center of the place is a man I've never seen before. We cautiously approach him as he stands calmly with five men behind him. There is something in my gut that feels off. He is short and stocky, with gray hair and a missing tooth.

"Are you the imbecile wasting my time?" I ask.

"I see the apple does not fall from the tree. Your father has no manners—it shouldn't surprise me that you don't either."

"You're still wasting my time," I warn with thin patience.

The man clears his throat. "You have something I want."

"What's that?"

"My niece."

Chapter 11

Lana

The muffled sounds of the wind outside are a chilling reminder of my isolation within the cold stone walls of this fortress. The air holds an oppressive silence, broken only by the distant sound of rain pattering against the roof. I stretch, my muscles stiff and weary from a restless night trapped in that pillory. My mind paints various scenarios of other possible torture devices Adrian may have around the house and how often will he inflict that onto me. I understand the predicament I am in, and either I can let it swallow me whole, or I can put up a fight.

"Ms. Petrova," a man with a disfigured face steps forward.

I hold back a gasp. "You must be Oslo."

A warm smile crosses his face as though he is grateful I'm not repulsed by him. "Should you need anything, I will be happy to get it for you. Adrian said to make sure you feel at home."

"Did he now?" I hold my hands in front of me and tilt my head. "I'd love to go to the flower shop. It would be nice to add some color around here."

"I'll bring the car around." Oslo bows his head before running off.

* * *

As I step out into the dampness, I feel a wave of determination wash over me. I need to take control, to secure my own safety amidst the uncertainty that looms like shadows. Oslo takes me to a specialty flower boutique that carries a variety of flowers and plants. As we pull up to the front, he has both hands tightly around the steering wheel. Watching his eyes look at the rearview mirror at himself, seeing him flinch a bit in disgust makes me want to cry for him. Unsure if he was born with a mutation or whether he suffered them while in prison, it is a clear reflection of his insecurities.

As much as I hope that he will stay in the car, I know he can't do that. Adrian said to make me feel at home but not to leave me unsupervised. Placing my hand onto his arm, I return the warm smile he gave me earlier. His body instantly relaxes. We quickly run into the boutique and shake off the rain.

"I'll be at the door whenever you're ready."

"Thank you, Oslo."

As I approach the register, I ding the bell three times. Out of the dark corner, a woman appears wearing the color yellow from head to toe.

"How can I help you?" She smiles from ear to ear.

"I'd like to know if you have any skeleton flowers."

She tilts her head slightly and nods. "They bloom beautifully on rainy days like this. Any special occasion?"

"I'd like to surprise my husband."

A sly smile takes over her face. "Right this way then."

Looking over my shoulder, Oslo is guarding the door. I follow the woman into the back of the shop to a hidden door. As we step into the private room, there are three rows of plants to choose from: a row of wolfsbane, a row of Volchya Yagoda, and a row of Belladonna.

"Pick your poison." The lady smirks. "If your husband is stupid, then I suggest the Belladonna. Let him pluck a berry himself to eat. Look how delicious these berries appear. Let him eat enough, and he can suffer a heart attack or fall into a coma."

"He's not stupid," I reply as I scan over the row of Volchya Yagoda.

"Has he used any of these before?"

I shrug. "Only you can answer that." Looking up at her, I ask, "Has Adrian or any Sokolovs been here before?"

The woman's face goes pale at the sound of Adrian's name. "You should never drop any names."

"I need you to know what I'm dealing with." I look to her as if to beg for help.

She brings me to the wolfsbane as she puts on rubber gloves. Picking from it, she holds it between us. "All parts of the plant are toxic, and the poison can be absorbed through the skin, so always wear gloves."

I nod my head. "How am I supposed to get it down his throat?"

"Crush it," she answers. "Put it in his food. Get creative."

"Will I get caught?"

"No," she confidently confirms. "The side effects from

ingesting or touching the plant are what will actually kill him. The autopsy will show death caused by refractory ventricular arrhythmias and ultimately cardiac arrest."

"Perfect." My eyes settle on a cluster of wolfsbane, its dark green leaves glistening with moisture, the violet flowers almost ethereal against the gloomy room. "I'll take one but have a bouquet of flowers wrapped around it so I can get it inside without suspicion."

"I have you covered. Don't worry. How do you think I've been able to keep this shop running with my lack of customers?" As she takes one of the plants, we walk back to the front of the shop. "How did you hear about me anyway?"

"What happened to not dropping names?" I side-eye her.

"Good," she nods. "You learn quick."

We reach the register, and the woman begins creating a large bouquet. After paying a hefty amount for the arrange-ment, she hands me a small packet of flower food as all florists do when purchasing a bouquet of flowers.

"Oh, no need," I decline as I don't intend to keep these flowers alive.

"In case you make a mistake, it's best to use within the first hour." She winks at me. "This is no joke."

Understanding this isn't flower food, I take the packet and look down at it. It reads *activated charcoal.*

"Thank you," I smile.

Oslo doesn't question a thing. Instead, he takes the large bouquet into the car and then into the house.

"Thank you, Oslo."

"Anytime, Ms. Petrova."

"Lana, please."

"Would you like to go anywhere else today?"

"If you can pick up a few things from the market, I'd like to make my husband some dinner."

Oslo makes no fuss and leaves me unattended. I waste no time disassembling the bouquet, pretending to split it up into smaller bouquets to place around the house. Once he sets foot out of the door, I take the wolfsbane and head to the kitchen.

The fortress seems to shift around me, each creak a reminder of Adrian's presence just a heartbeat away. The promise of empowerment tingles at my fingertips. I am no longer a passive occupant of his world. I am becoming a fortress of my own making.

Taking a butcher's knife, I begin chopping the plant and its leaves into tiny pieces. When I am done, I stare at it, realizing how much I actually have. Placing a portion of it into a plate to use as an herb to marinate dinner, I quickly scan the kitchen to find other ways to hide pieces of the wolfsbane. Opening a cupboard, there are tea bags, and a lightbulb goes off. Taking a full packet, I remove the herbs from the tea bags and replace them with the chopped wolfsbane. Neatly placing each tea bag back into the packet, I breathe a sigh of relief. I have taken the first steps toward reclaiming my power, constructing my defenses with the resources nature provides.

Focusing back on the disassembled bouquet, I make about five mini bouquets of flowers and place them around the house.

"I'm back!" Oslo shouts. "I'll place the groceries in the kitchen."

"Thank you!" I shout as I place the last bouquet on a console placed in the hallway.

As I make my way to the kitchen, I see Oslo standing in

front of the plate of finely chopped wolfsbane and tossing it into the trash.

"What are you doing?" I ask as I rush toward him.

"That was some kind of expired herb. Where did you get that?" he asks as he holds his hand to his head.

Panic sets in. "I was looking for spices. I forgot to list one."

"Top cupboard over there," Oslo points as he slightly stumbles.

"Are you okay?" My body begins to sweat.

"I'm really dizzy. Everything is blurry."

I help him to a seat. "I'll get you water."

"Strange. I lightly patted some of the spice onto my tongue. Who knew expired spices would cause this."

Should I let him die? Yes. Can I let him die? My heart can't allow it. He has been respectful and kind to me. He doesn't deserve this. Oslo is beginning to sweat as he holds his head up for support.

"Let me make you something my grandmother taught me. You should feel better soon."

Sprinting to find the activated charcoal, I rip it open and dump it into the water. Oslo doesn't even notice a thing and drinks the liquid without questioning it.

"This doesn't taste good," he coughs as the powder isn't thoroughly mixed with the water.

"Trust me. You need to drink the whole thing." I hold the glass up to his mouth, making sure he drinks every last drop of it.

Slowly, Oslo seems to start coming to his senses but still looks like he got hit by a bus.

"I'm going to lie down. My apologies that I can't take you anywhere else."

"It's okay," I manage to smile. "Do you need help?"

"No, no. I'm fine."

Oslo slowly makes his way out of the kitchen. I grab the edge of the counter with both hands as I lean forward, taking a deep breath. The woman wasn't lying—this is no joke. The rest of the wolfsbane is safely tucked away in the tea bags. For now, I will bide my time, watch, and wait, ready to fend off any wrath that Adrian may unleash before I fully commit to this.

Chapter 12

Adrian

I return home just after eight pm, exhausted, dirty, and angry. Ready to call it a day, I remove my shirt stained with blood and dirt as I head toward my wing of the house. A scent catches my attention, and I head in its direction. I find myself in the kitchen.

Leaning against the polished wood of the door frame, my eyes narrow as I watch Lana move deftly around the kitchen. Her graceful movements, as she hums softly to herself, stirring the bubbling pot on the stove, the savory aroma wafts through the air. I can smell garlic and herbs mingling with something earthy and rich, creating a tempting scent that makes my stomach rumble. But I'm not hungry. Not really. Not with the shadows of betrayal lurking at the edges of my mind. At the end of the day, she is still a Petrova, an enemy living under my roof.

I clear my throat, the sound sharp in the stillness of the kitchen. "What is this?"

She seems startled by my voice. "You're back."

Walking toward her, I grab a butcher's knife along the way, letting it drag against the countertop as I approach her. "You didn't answer my question."

"I-I'm making dinner," she stutters as her eyes remain glued to the knife. "I'm making Solyanka."

"Solyanka?" I repeat, the words laced with suspicion. Did she know that was a favorite dish of mine? "Why?"

She arches her brow. "Should I stay in the bedroom until you're ready for a fuck?"

She hitches her breath when I place the tip of the butcher knife at her throat. "Where's Oslo?"

"He wasn't feeling well," she gulps. "I'm almost done if you're hungry."

It is difficult to get out of this dark mindset after getting my hands dirty. I take a moment, then step back. "Go ahead." I give her permission to continue and stand beside the counter to watch her.

I watch her chop vegetables, her knife glinting in the low light, and a dark thought creeps into my mind: What if she is poisoning me? I have tangled with enough people in my life to know that something as simple as dinner can become a deadly game. Years in the Bratva have mercilessly taught me that trust can be a fatal flaw.

"You understand, if you poison me, there will be no one to save you. The men here will eat you alive."

Lana's laughter rings through the kitchen, sweet yet dangerous, filling the space with a mix of tension and curiosity. "Poison you? That's a rather extreme assumption, don't you think?" She steps closer, her regained confidence radiating even as I maintain my guarded posture. "What would I gain from killing you? I have nowhere to go and no one to go to."

"Your deceased father, mother, and husband are three

reasons." I step closer, my eyes boring into hers, searching for a crack in her composure.

She tilts her head, unfazed. "If you think I'd poison you, perhaps that says more about you than it does about me."

A low growl of frustration escapes me. Grabbing the chain around her neck, I yank it down. "You're playing a dangerous game, Lana."

"I'm just making dinner. You can have some or you don't."

Taking the knife, I lightly place the point onto her throat again.

"You have an uncle. Igor."

She remains silent, causing me to push the end of the sharp knife further into her throat until I see the fear in her eyes.

"I haven't seen him in years."

"Well, he knew where to find you." The whisper escapes my mouth. "He's not coming to save you."

I feel a hand wrap around the hand that is gripping the knife. "I had nothing to do with him coming here."

My phone rings, and my free hand pulls it out of my pocket. "What?" My eyes never leave Lana's.

"He's not a threat," Sergei informs. "He's not here to save the girl, just wants access to the railroad. Apparently, the Petrovi family was part of a private railroad being built to transport products underground that would run from Western Europe to China. It would ensure products were being moved safely and discreetly."

"Secure the connection, then drop the dead weight." I hang up and drag the tip of the knife down her bruised neck and onto her chest. "Should I expect anyone else coming to save you?" Does she hope she will be saved?

Lana shakes her head. "I have no one."

I need to make a statement that is loud and clear. "I'll make sure of that."

Chapter 13

Lana

I stand at the altar, my hands trembling as I clutch the bouquet of white orchids. The soft fabric of my wedding gown is draped gracefully over my curvy frame, the intricate lace hugging my hips. My thick hair is swept up in an elegant style, a few stray strands framing my round face. At the front of the church, waiting at the altar, stands Adrian, the man who has taken everything from me. His dark hair is neatly combed, his sharp features exuding an air of confidence and power. He's wearing an expensive tailored suit, his broad shoulders filling it out perfectly. Adrian's gaze is intense, his eyes piercing through anyone who dares to meet them. He is a man who commands attention, and today, he is claiming his prize—me.

The guests, a mix of wealthy elites and feared gangsters, fill the pews. They whisper amongst themselves, aware of the significance of this union. I, the daughter of the late crime boss, am being wedded to Adrian, the ruthless man who has solidified power by killing my entire family. It is a marriage born out of fear and coercion.

As I take each step toward him, my heart pounds in my chest. I feel like a sacrificial lamb being led to the slaughter. It feels like a dream; I lose my family, and now, I marry their killer to ensure my safety. Adrian was right because shortly after the news broke of my father's death, there was a bounty placed on my head. I heard the housemaids talking about it all day yesterday. My father had enemies from everywhere, both criminal and political figures. He was untouchable until Adrian set his mind to taking him down. The weight of emotion pushes down on my chest.

Reaching the altar, I stand beside him, our bodies almost touching. I can feel his warmth, his raw masculinity, and it sends shivers down my spine. The priest begins the ceremony, his words echoing in the grand hall.

"Now face one another," the priest directs us.

The priest's words blur together as dread pools in the pit of my stomach. I can barely hear a word as I try to remain calm. His eyes never leave my face, his intense stare making me blush despite being under my veil. There is no denying he's desirable, but I loathe him more. The only reason he spared my life was the phone call he received. It makes me wonder if Adrian is really the one in charge.

The vows are spoken, and as he slips the wedding ring onto my finger, his rough fingers graze my skin, sending a jolt through my body. I can't help but notice the contrast between our hands—mine small and delicate, and his large, tattooed and calloused. He holds my hands possessively, his thumb stroking my skin, leaving a trail of goose bumps in its wake.

"I now pronounce you husband and wife," the priest declares, and the guests clap in unison.

We stand side by side on display for all to witness this union. Getting a better look at the crowd, I notice the most prominent oligarchs amidst criminals. It isn't surprising as the oligarchy here is losing their power and needs men of the bratva as their muscle. Adrian turns around to face me, pulling out something from his pocket, a thick Cuban chain with a hollow heart on one end and a solid heart on the other that he wraps around my neck. Holding one end of the necklace that has the solid heart, he pushes it through the hollow heart on the end of the other side, then pulls on it so that it tightly wraps around my neck like a choker. This is it. I am now a Sokolov—a caged bird on display.

Adrian leans in, his lips brushing against my ear. "You're mine now," he whispers in a threat that sends shivers down my spine.

The burning of vomit erupts up my throat as he pulls on the chain, forcing me to move. Walking down the aisle, I look like a dog on a leash. He is making a statement, not just to me but to everyone in the room watching. Just outside is a white Aurus Senat limousine waiting for us. My eyes begin to water as people watch him practically drag me into the vehicle. I know this isn't going to be a blissful marriage, but I am hoping to at least be treated as a human being. While trapped in that pillory overnight, I contemplated taking my own life, but I refuse to give Adrian that kind of satisfaction.

The driver opens the door, and the chain tightens around my neck as Adrian yanks me forward so that I get into the car first. Stepping into the plush interior of the limousine, the scent of leather mingles with the faint aroma of my bouquet, which I toss on an empty seat. The door clicks shut behind me as though sealing me into this gilded cage. As I adjust my wedding gown, a swirl of white lace that feels foreign against my skin, I refuse to acknowledge

Adrian sitting beside me and turn to look out at the city of Moscow as we begin to move.

The streets are alive with energy, but I feel like a ghost. Gazing through the tinted glass, I watch buildings glide past. The golden domes of St. Basil's, the stark façade of the Kremlin, are all looming symbols of my entrapment. Each landmark is a reminder of the life I had just two days ago, one that had swirled away like the smoke from the car's exhaust.

Adrian sits beside me, a granite statue of power in a tailored suit, his posture stiff and proper.

"You know," he begins, his voice low and smooth, "this marriage means you'll be expected to uphold the Sokolov name with grace and poise."

I turn my head slightly, allowing my disdain to bubble to the surface. "Is that with the leash or without?"

His gray taunting eyes flick toward me as if evaluating whether to take it personally or let the sarcasm slide. "Don't take it so personally. Learn to properly behave, and I won't need the leash."

"Is that all it takes not to be treated like a pet?"

He smirks, unfazed by my retort. "You'll learn to enjoy the privileges that come with being my wife. You'll have access to the finest things: clothes, jewelry, experiences. More importantly, my protection. You should feel fortunate."

"Fortunate?" I echo incredulously. "You think I want to wear pretty dresses while you make a mockery of me?"

He leans toward me, a hint of amusement creeping into his expression. "You'll learn, Lana. This is your new life. Spare yourself the energy to rebel. You're part of something much bigger now. Remember, obedience is key. I've made sacrifices for this union. You owe me loyalty."

He isn't wrong, I know that. He spared my life for his own benefit, but I gained something as well—power. It may not be as strong as his, but it's more than what I would have gotten if I didn't agree to this marriage. I turn my gaze back toward the window, watching as a crowd of older teenagers parades down the street, their laughter echoing in the air.

"Will it always be like this?" I whisper to myself, but Adrian catches the challenge.

His laughter is cold, devoid of warmth. "You'll adapt. You have no choice."

The air around me is heavy and suffocating. I feel the weight of his words settle in my chest like a stone, but within me grows a flicker of determination. I will endure this, survive it, perhaps even escape it. Through the shimmering cityscape, I still feel a glimmer of hope waiting for me somewhere, hidden among the shadows of my new reality. A soft sigh escapes my lips, a silent vow echoing in the bleakness. One day, I will reclaim my freedom.

Chapter 14

Adrian

"What exactly do you want, Vlad?"

"Adrian, I need you to get rid of the prime minister."

"It will cost you triple for conducting business on his wedding day," Sergei voices as he stands behind Moscow's most elite oligarch.

"I will pay whatever price," Vladimir replies, looking straight at me.

"How do you benefit from his death?" I question as I hold a gun in my hand, my arm hanging to my side.

"You mean, how do we benefit from it," Vladimir challenges. "The prime minister plans to secure borders by strict inspection of all cargo going in and out of Russia. I know that will present a challenge for you."

Stepping closer, I watch him hold his breath in my presence, making me hold back a laugh. "I appreciate you looking out for us." The sarcasm rolls off my tongue. "There are other ways I can get my products moved around, secure border or not."

"This is personal," he lets out a light exhale. "He plans to take the majority of my territories as punishment for my daughter refusing to give her hand in marriage to his son."

A knock at the door interrupts the conversation.

"Think about it," Vladimir says, walking toward the door. "I would be indebted to you."

As he leaves, Ivan comes in. "Your wife has been seated alone this entire reception, refusing to mingle."

"Don't look so disgusted," Sergei replies to him, lighting up a cigarette as he takes a seat.

"You didn't have to stand in front of an audience witnessing a fake marriage," I rub my chin roughly.

Sergei lets out a laugh. "It's not fake, it's legitimate."

I walk over to a window that overlooks the outside of the venue. "I should lock her in a tower like Ivan had suggested."

Ivan lets out a hearty laugh. "She's not bad looking, and it won't be so bad having a pussy to stuff your cock into whenever you want." He takes a chug of his liquor, trying to further convince me that having her around is beneficial. "Plus, I had what was left over of dinner last night; she knows how to cook. So, you get a full stomach as well."

"I would assume so at her weight." The words leave my mouth unashamed.

"More cushion for the pushing." Ivan smirks and shoots me a wink.

Although I despise her for being a Petrova, it irks me hearing Ivan speak of her. I know he will never cross that line, so why do my nerves tick at the thought, getting me even more annoyed.

"Beats jerking off alone in a dark, cold cell." Sergei lets out a cloud of smoke.

"Exactly. Pussy whenever you want it." Ivan raises his bottle in salute.

"Get her in here," I reply, grabbing the nearest bottle of vodka and chugging it.

As I wait, I stand by the grand window of the lavish suite, the city lights of Moscow twinkling like stars across the skyline and adjust my cufflinks, the cool metal a stark contrast to the warmth radiating from the room.

The door opens and in walks Sergei. "The new Mrs. Sokolov."

Behind him walks Lana, her silhouette framed by the dim light behind her. She is a vision in her elegant gown, delicate lace cascading down her body like a waterfall, but there is an unmistakable tightness in the way she holds herself. After locking her in that room, she seems shaken around me. The nervous energy radiating from her is palpable, and it sparks an odd, fierce protective instinct within me.

"Are you not having fun at our wedding?"

She hesitates, fingers nervously twisting the delicate fabric of her dress. Her wide eyes, usually so confident and fierce, are replaced with a flicker of vulnerability that I had not anticipated.

"There is nothing worth celebrating," she replies softly, avoiding eye contact.

I walk to her and watch as she tenses the closer I get. I tug on the chain that tightened around her neck, causing her to gasp and finally look at me.

"Be a good girl and put on a smile before I have to carve one into your face," I politely inform her.

"Your mother told me to keep to myself," she gulps,

gripping her hands around my forearm as though that will loosen my grip. Her eyes widen with a plea for restraint.

"You are married to me and therefore will follow only my commands. Is that understood?"

"Yes," she replies.

I can feel her heart pulsing quickly against my fist that lies against her chest. Each beat sends a wave of pleasure right to my cock.

"Leave us," I command Ivan and Sergei.

They exit, and there is a shift in the room. Lana is breathing heavier; I can feel her nerves kicking up. The silence is so deadly; the sound of her heart pounding against her chest vibrates through her skin, sending a bolt of excitement through me.

"On your knees, wife." My lips curl into a faint smirk.

"Needy already?"

I pull on the chain further, causing the metal to tightly wrap around her neck, inflicting enough pain for her skin to turn red, only allowing her to take in small breaths of air. Slowly, she lowers herself while holding onto my forearm for balance. Kneeling on the plush carpet, hands resting on her thighs, she is the picture of obedience.

"Look at me," I command.

Lana's eyes flicker up to meet mine, her irises a deep shade of brown that seem to swallow the light.

"You understand your purpose as my wife, don't you?" I ask in a tone laced with a mixture of amusement and cruelty.

She swallows hard. "Yes," she whispers, her voice barely audible. Her hands tremble slightly, but she keeps them firmly planted on her thighs, as if to anchor herself.

"Say it."

She tries to take a deep breath, her chest heaving slightly. "To please you," she murmurs.

Reaching into my suit pants, I pull out my cock. Still holding onto the chain, I begin stroking myself with my free hand until it is fully erect and ready to be satisfied.

"Go ahead, open up." I reach out, my fingers tangling in her perfectly styled hair, pulling her head back slightly so she is forced to look at me. When she doesn't, I smirk. "Do you need a reminder on the consequences of disobedience?" My voice is devoid of emotion.

There is a flicker of hate in her eyes as her lips part over the head of my cock. I grip the back of her head and guide her forward. She resists for a moment, her lips brushing against me, causing a slight shiver of sensation down my leg. I push her head down, forcing my cock into her mouth.

She gags softly, her eyes watering as she struggles to adjust to the intrusion. I hold her firmly, my grip unyielding, as I take over and begin to thrust into her mouth. The warmth and softness cause my cock to involuntarily throb in pleasure. She tries to keep up with my pace, her tongue flicking over my shaft, her lips moving in rhythm. I don't care about her comfort, only my own pleasure.

"Keep up," I mutter in disdain.

Lana's cheeks hollow as she tries to take me deeper, her hands clenched into fists. My thrusts grow more forceful, my breath coming in sharp gasps. I'm not making love to her —I am using her, and this should have made her hate me; however, it seems as though she is enjoying this just as much as I am. Feeling the tension through my body as the buildup accumulates, I let out a growl as my cum shoots out with one final thrust. I hear her choke lightly.

"Swallow it, you fucking whore. Every last drop."

My cock pumps out my semen in what feels like loads

until my balls feel light again. Pulling away, my cock slips from her mouth with a wet pop. As I adjust myself, Lana stands up in front of me, eyes wet from tears. All of a sudden, my face is drenched as I feel a thick goo all over my skin. The bitch spits my cum onto my face. Jolting my arm forward, I cup her jaw tightly.

"You're going to pay for that."

Chapter 15

Lana

After waiting an hour alone in the empty room, the door rips open.

"Follow me," Adrian demands, holding a gun at his side.

As I let Adrian take the lead out of the room, Ivan and Sergei follow behind me. We walk out to the room, down the hall, and out the back doors of the venue in complete silence. There is a gust of wind that causes goosebumps to crawl all over my skin. Adrian stops once we hit a dirt path. There is an eerie feeling that's unsettling. As I step forward beside him, the most horrific sight I have ever seen is displayed for me.

Adrian kisses the side of my temple and then marvels at the display. "Next time you spit something in my face, it will be your head on a pike."

I scream in horror as I look at three heads on spikes, their blood still dripping onto the ground. One holds my father, the second holds my mother, and the third holds my ex-husband. The weight of distress presses down on me as tears blur my eyes. I fall to my knees as the struggle inside me is fierce, a battle between grief and hate for the man I just married.

"Let this be a lesson, Lana. As my wife, I will protect you, but the outcome of your actions will determine how I deliver my kindness."

There's a rupture of madness that shakes within me, and before I can process my thoughts, I lunge at Adrian. Repeatedly hitting him in the chest, but he barely moves.

"I hate you!" I scream. "How could you be so cruel!? Have you no shame!?"

Ivan and Sergei are about to rip me off him, but Adrian waves for them to stand back. They stand there watching me spiral. Adrian takes both my wrists into his one hand, spins me around, and pulls me into him as he holds a gun to my head with his other hand. My back is against his chest as he holds my wrists tightly against my breasts to keep me in place.

"Your husband always bragged about how tight you were," he growls, his breath hot on my neck.

"Fuck you!" I spit out.

This only seems to fuel his excitement. His erection grows against the crack of my ass. He spins me around to face him.

"Undress yourself," he says, his voice low and husky.

"No," I reply. "I'll never give myself willingly to you."

One side of his mouth curves into a smile. "It doesn't have to be willingly." He holds the gun to my face.

My heart races as I feel the full force of his desire. If I fight him, I can only imagine what he will do to me, but when I see my family on display like trophies, I don't even think twice and begin to run. At the force of stomping my foot into the ground, my heel gets stuck in the dirt, causing me to fall forward, right onto my face. Quickly trying to push myself to my knees, I feel the weight of a heavy hand against my back push me back onto the dirt, stealing all the breath from my lungs. The earthy scent of cold dirt rushes into my nose, mixed with his spicy citrus cologne, suffocating me. Dirt cakes under my fingernails as I attempt to crawl out of his hold. It's useless once he pins me under his hard body, the muscles of his chest and thighs tense against my frame as he holds the gun to my temple.

I lie there, breathing heavily as he rolls his hips, grinding his thick cock in between my ass cheeks. Adrian flips me over as though I am as light as a feather.

Pointing the gun to my forehead, his deep voice spills out. "That was a stupid move."

Tracing the gun down my face, over my chin, sliding down my neck as he hovers over me. His dark eyes smolder with intensity, his free hand planted on the ground right beside my head, propping himself up. Keeping the gun close to my head, he falls onto me so that our mouths collide with a demanding kiss. His tongue invades my mouth with a hunger that mirrors his character. I taste the sweetness of vodka on his breath, mixed with the bitterness of our circumstances. His hand roams freely over my body, tracing the curves of my waist and hips. The gun is being held at my temple once again. I look to the side and see his two men watching.

Adrian grabs my chin and yanks it centered so we are eye to eye. "Why don't you boys take a walk?"

I hear their footsteps trail away. This is my reward for obeying. His hands tug at the delicate fabric of my gown, tearing it slightly as he exposes my breasts. I gasp as his mouth latches onto the sensitive peak, sucking and teasing it with his tongue. His hands travel down my body, caressing my thick thighs, making me squirm. In a moment of impulse, he rips the dress completely off my body. His hand in between my thighs makes its way to my lace underwear, in which he wastes no time ripping through it with his fingers and then stroking me intimately.

"You make it hard to believe you hate me," he murmurs, his voice thick with desire against my mouth.

I hold back from lashing out at him. Lifting himself onto his knees, he quickly removes his pants, then his body falls back onto me in a swift movement. He enters me with one swift thrust with a possessiveness that matches his nature. I arch my back, crying out as he fills me completely, his hard body driving into my soft flesh. My body sinks further into the dirt as Adrian's pace quickens, his breath coming in ragged gasps. He fucks me with a primal urgency, his hands gripping my hips, leaving marks on my pale skin. My nails dig into his shoulders as though urging him on. It's a mix of hate and lust, whirled in a moment of complete vulnerability. The more he thrusts inside me, the more it aches and burns. He gives me no time to adjust to the size of his cock, which he is rutting into me like a wild animal.

"Tell me you want more," he growls.

When I refuse, the harder he pounds inside of me, he hits my cervix, causing me to gasp for air.

"More," I grit through my teeth.

"Louder!"

"More!!" I shout as loudly as possible.

This drives him wild, and he pounds into me with wildness, his cock throbbing inside me. It feels as though he's going to rip me open. My body trembles as my orgasm builds, my senses overwhelmed by the raw pleasure he is giving me. As he's claiming my body, the sky darkens ominously, and soon enough, light droplets fall from the clouds, adding intensity to this moment.

"Bozhe moy!" My last cry of pleasure as my orgasm hits me like a wave, my body convulsing beneath him. Adrian follows, his powerful thrusts becoming erratic as he spills his release deep within me. We lie entangled, breathless and sweaty, our hearts pounding in unison—mine from this intrusive invasion of personal space, while his must be from the excitement of the moment.

"That's a good girl," he says as a devilish, handsome smirk crosses his face that makes my stomach turn.

If he sees me crumble in front of him, he will know he's won. "Is that all you got?"

"It's just a taste," he licks off a drop of rain that lands on the top of my nose, "wife."

Chapter 16

Adrian

"**A**drian," my father's voice travels from behind me as I walk back into the venue. "I need a word."

I let him follow me into a private area away from guests. "What is it?"

Ignoring my annoyance, he asks, "Why do you look disheveled? You have dirt all over your clothes. Where's your bride?"

"That's not your concern," I reply, not letting him know that Sergei and Ivan are watching her mourn her family display outside. "What do you need?"

"You always assume I need something."

"That's because you always do," I remind him.

"The seizure of the Volga Diamond should have been clean and smooth. Instead, I'm told there is a pending investigation, and I am their top suspect."

"It was smooth, but to think it would have been a clean operation is laughable.—I should have known the eerie silence after the Volga Diamond's takeover was a bad sign. I just figured the moles inside the police station were keeping it under wraps."

He clenches his fists. "Get it under wraps." He pulls something out of the inside of his suit jacket. "There's something else."

He hands me a single, unmarked envelope, its plain white surface devoid of any identifying marks. Inside it, I find a single playing card—the Queen of Spades—folded neatly, accompanied by a typewritten note: "The game is far from over, Boris. Your reign will end soon."

The Queen of Spades. A chilling symbol and an indication of misfortune. I trace the edges of the card with my calloused finger, while my mind races. The message is stark, a contrast to the sadistic threats of our adversaries. This is the work of someone calculating, someone with resources far beyond the reach of the petty criminals I've dealt with thus far. It is a message from a different level of the game, a player whose existence I haven't suspected.

"When did you get this?" I ask.

"This morning." I see fear boring through his eyes.

"And you bring it to my attention now?" my voice irate.

"I didn't want to put bad karma right before the wedding ceremony."

"You mean you didn't want me to change my mind."

"Securing the Volkov resources solidifies and secures our power here and outside the city."

I let out a huff. "Power is the only thing you ever care about."

He grabs my shoulders, gripping them with such intensity as though it will make me understand better. "You were sent to prison for taking out all our rivals. Letting that girl live was a smart move. She's your alibi. The rumor is that she came to you for solace. If the police get ahold of you for anything, you will be put away for good, and there's nothing I will be able to do about it. You were supposed to get life, and it was a miracle when your appeal for a shorter sentence was granted. I couldn't risk it. Losing you again. You're the glue that holds this family together. I will leave this to you. You're in charge now."

As I nod my head, my father pats my back. A gust of wind enters the room when one of the doors is opened, and Lana comes speed walking in with Ivan and Sergei behind her. When she sees us standing there looking at her, she bows her head in submission.

"What happened to your dress?" my father asks with disgust.

She stands there with a torn and muddy dress, with her face of smudged makeup and puffy eyes. "I tripped," she replies.

"Go into the restroom and clean yourself up," I demand.

We watch Lana enter the bridal suite in silence.

"You'll have your hands full with that one," my father comments.

"Let me deal with that. In the meantime, tell mother never to command my wife again."

With a contorted face, he replies, "Your mother would never."

"She has, and knowing her, she won't stop unless you tell her to."

"Alright, I'll speak with her. In the meantime, find out who sent that." He points to the envelope, then turns and walks away.

Once he's out of sight, I turn to Ivan and Sergei.

"Looks like someone is looking for trouble," I say, handing them the envelope.

Chapter 17

Lana

Walking into the restroom, I check every stall before I crumble into pieces. The weight of my gown feels like chains wrapped around my body, dragging me down. I still feel him on my skin; his cock leaves a beating pulse in my core; his scent sticks to me. There is no shaking him off, but that isn't the most disturbing thing—why did my body enjoy every second of it? Am I going crazy? As I fight back the tide of emotions, anger, humiliation, and disbelief take over me. I rush to the sink, splashing cold water onto my face, but it only intensifies the fire in my chest. The scent of antiseptic stings my nostrils, mixing with the delicate smell of flowers that were picked out for the event. A sob escapes my throat, raw and feral. I didn't pick out anything for today. Not the venue, not the décor, not even the dress. Everything was planned and picked out by Adrian's mother.

The lighting of the bathroom reflects off the marble tiles, illuminating the tear streaks on my face. As I lean over onto the countertop, gripping the edge, as waves of rage course through me like electricity, I fight the urge to break the vase and slit my own throat. Just as my mind goes blank, someone walks into the restroom. I hear the sound of heels rhythmically clicking against the tile. I look up into the mirror and see Raya.

"Lana? Are you okay?" Her voice is low and cautious. She leans against the wall, eyes glinting as if she can see through the despair.

Despite the circumstances, I feel a flicker of warmth from Raya's presence. "I'm fine."

Raya steps closer. "They are a tough crowd." Her hazel eyes soften the closer she gets to me. "If you want to talk about it..."

I turn to face her. "There's nothing to say that could make this better."

"Adrian is...he takes time to get used to." She places one of her hands on her hip. "It took them a long time to let me in after Gil and I were together."

"Gil seems more at ease. I'm sure he is a lot easier to handle."

Raya smiles. "They come from the same sperm. Apple doesn't fall too far from the tree." She takes a deep breath. "I'm sure if Gil spent five years of his life, surviving the Black Dolphin, he wouldn't be so laid back."

"You're trying to make me feel better about this marriage. I'm sure you have your own doubts."

I'm not sure if Raya is convinced this marriage is made on the security of survival and power.

"Doesn't matter what I think." Raya's hand falls off her hip, and her hands come together in front of her. "But here's some advice. Keep your head low and out of Adrian's way.

You can make this marriage work in your own twisted way. You barely need to be around him unless he says so."

"I'd rather know what sets him off."

Raya laughs. "You're feisty. You sure you want to explore that?"

"Without a doubt."

Chapter 18

Adrian

"Her tits were the size of two watermelons." Ivan motions with his hands as he details his last conquest.

"Real or fake?" Sergei questions.

"Fake. They weren't as soft as real ones."

"Not my thing. I prefer them real, big or small, doesn't matter."

"That wasn't the craziest part."

I listen and laugh at the conversation between the two. We are seated on plush chairs, each with a bottle of liquor and an ashtray in the center. It almost mimicked when we would be on prison grounds, just bullshitting to make the day go by faster. The only difference is that instead of concrete floors, we are on white velvet plush chairs placed on mahogany wood floors, dressed in designer clothes, and drinking the best vodka money can buy.

Sergei puts out his cigarette and lights up another. "Girl had watermelon-sized tits and a tattoo of her father's name on her pussy. The only way it can get crazier is if she had a penis."

"No penis. But she did something that I've never experienced before, and I'm not complaining about it." Ivan shrugs.

"What new kink are you into now, you dirty pig?"

"She was sucking my dick, I mean slurping, drooling, gagging, the works. She was going hard. All I said was 'That's right, take this dick,' and she just stops." Ivan gestures with his hand as he speaks. "She looks up at me and says, 'I'm in control here.' It was cute, and so I laughed." Ivan shakes his head in defeat as he proceeds with his story. "She throws my legs up over my head and goes right at it. Attacking my asshole with her tongue."

Sergei's eyes widen. "What the fuck, Ivan!?"

I can't contain myself and bust out laughing, barely able to breathe. Ivan joins in while Sergei is still wrapping his head around what Ivan just told us.

A knock on the door interrupts us.

"Come in!" I shout.

Gil opens the door and stumbles in. "Brother! I haven't drunk this much alcohol since my own wedding. Only you would be hiding from the crowd at your own wedding."

Ivan rolls his eyes, and Sergei lights up a cigarette.

"If you're still standing, then you haven't drunk enough," I shoot back.

"Well, I can't get too crazy. Who else will look after your new wife?" Gil slumps onto a chair and kicks his feet up onto the coffee table.

"What are you talking about, Gil?"

"Lana and Oliver Braylov seem to be getting very friendly by the bar."

Jealousy snakes its way through my thoughts, wrapping

around my chest like a vice. This may not be a marriage based on love, but it sure as hell won't make a mockery out of me. Once a woman is married, they have no reason to speak to other men unless their spouse is present.

"Must not be so bad if you're here," I reply.

Gil shrugged. "I told Raya to distract her."

My nostrils flare. "Your wife doesn't have the best reputation around men."

"She's behaved since we got married. Plus, I can't be too upset when I have my own side entertainment. It's more of an unspoken mutual agreement."

I shoot Sergei a glance, and he knows exactly what he needs to do. My eyes dart to Ivan, who simply nods and gets to his feet.

"Enjoy the rest of the night." I get to my feet as well.

"You're leaving?" Gil stumbles onto his feet. "It's not even midnight."

"I'm tired."

"Don't fall asleep on your new bride. You'll want to make it a memorable night."

I huff. "No need to worry about making good impressions."

* * *

Lana remains silent as she sits beside me, but there's an air of attitude that I wouldn't have expected after how I treated her. She's tougher than I imagined she would be. Part of that excites me, but I'm not sure if it is the challenge of breaking her into pieces or the admiration of her resilience.

"How's Oliver?"

"Who?" she asks with a convincing innocence.

"The man you happen to entertain at our wedding."

"You said to mingle," she shoots back. "You didn't put a restriction on with whom."

Snatching the hanging chain from her and yanking it toward me so that her face is right up against mine, the fear radiates off her, but she remains calm and collected.

"You're smart enough to know what I meant."

"What are you going to do about it?" her voice laced with mockery.

Tugging on the chain some more, I can see her neck muscles moving as she tries to breathe. I can put her back in the pillory, but I think she actually will enjoy that.

Pulling her closer so our lips practically brush against each other, we lock into a stare. "I could cut that tongue out of your mouth so you'd never be able to speak again."

I feel her mouth curve up into a smile. "Then how will I be able to please you?" Her hand grabs my cock, making it twitch.

"You think I can't find someone else to do that?" I grab her hand and rip it off me but still hold on to it. "Don't think you're that special."

"You wouldn't dare mutilate me. You need me just as much as I need you." She licks the point of my nose, the same gesture I had done to her after claiming her body in front of her dead family.

We are in a stare off, our breathing in opposite rhythms.

"What makes you think I won't?"

Her free hand touches my chest, and she slides it up to my shoulder and wraps her hands around the back of my neck.

"You want this to look like a legitimate marriage. You need everyone to think we are in love and that I allow you to have complete control over me."

"That's a bold assumption."

"But I'm not wrong, am I?"

She is looking to have the upper hand, and to be honest, she always does hold the upper hand. I just don't want her to know that for this very reason; she will use it against me, and I hate for anyone to have something to hold over my head or think they have power over me.

"What if you're wrong?" I propose.

"If I were, you'd be holding my tongue in your hand."

The fierce look in her eyes and the confident tone in her voice sets my nerves on fire and sends a bolt of electricity to my cock.

Letting go of her hand and cupping her chin with the knuckle of my pointer finger, I ask, "Are you able to handle playing along?"

"I survived the last 48 hours with you. I think I'll manage just fine."

I try holding back a smile and accidentally brush my lips against hers. It gives me a strong urge for more skin-on-skin contact. Instead of giving in to temptation, I push her away.

"Do you have any terms you want me to consider?" I ask, turning this arrangement into a business transaction.

"I only ask to be treated like a human, not just in front of others, but behind closed doors as well." She adjusts her dress.

"I have specific needs. If you can't fill them, then a prostitute will."

"I'll satisfy all of your needs without you having to force yourself onto me. Can you manage that?"

"You're playing with fire," I warn her.

"You're the one who lit the match."

I roll up the sleeves of my shirt as it suddenly feels hot in here. "I suppose you want to get rid of the necklace."

She places her hand onto the chain around her neck. "I actually rather like it."

Chapter 19

Lana

Opening my eyes to a dark room, my nerves kick in. Half thankful I'm alive, while half terrified of the day ahead of me. Raya gave me good advice, and I plan to use it all to my advantage. Until things get completely out of hand, I'll save my tea bags for when I know my life is in absolute danger. After seeing how Oslo reacted to a small amount of the wolfsbane, I am slightly traumatized. I hear heavy breathing, yet when I roll onto my back, I don't see anyone lying beside me. Immediately, I sit up on the bed, checking my surroundings. The room is a canvas of shadows, almost completely blacked out, except for the piercing shafts of sunlight that fight valiantly through the sides of the shades, desperate to cast light on this oppressive gloom.

I check the floor beside me, its wooden surface cold and uninviting, but no one is there. Crawling to the other side of the king-size bed, I look down at a body on the floor. Adrian lies face down in his briefs with no blanket or pillow, fast asleep. His biceps flex as his head rests on one of his forearms, while the other is beside his head, his plump lips slightly parted. My eyes watch as the perfectly sculpted back muscles rise up and down with his breathing. Each breath he takes seems to bring the dark room to life, accentuating the powerful muscles beneath his skin. He is all muscle and tattooed from neck to toe. How can such a monster look so heavenly? Lowering my head to examine the artwork on his skin, I notice scars etched into his skin. He seems to have battle wounds almost everywhere.

A deep sigh that escapes his mouth startles me, and I lie back onto the bed. Quietly, I try to control my breathing, but when I feel a hand grab my arm, I gasp. Before I know it, I'm being pulled onto the floor and fall onto his torso, face to face.

"Morning, wife."

His deep voice is calm as I lie on his hard body. His eyelids slightly open, those gray eyes peak through, holding a sultry look of desire. His growing erection is looking to be satisfied. Adrian rolls over so he is on top of me, placing his hand behind my head to serve as a pillow. My hands immediately make their way to his chest, the palms of my hands pushing on his pecks as though that will stop his advances. I know resistance is a dangerous bet, so I surrender to him, letting my eyes flutter closed as his lips descend upon mine.

Lowering his head, he starts kissing my cheekbone and making his way to my jawline, down to my neck. Somehow, his erection is still growing as I feel it on my bare thigh. My body is tingling despite how much I want to resist him. Lifting his head so that our noses touch, we lock eyes. The sultry look is replaced with anger, as though he is expecting to see someone else.

Lifting his body off mine, Adrian flips me onto my stomach. My hands that were on his chest are now on the hardwood floor. Feeling his body hovering over mine, he whispers into my ear.

"I like to start my mornings with empty ball sacks."

With that said, I feel the delicate lace of my thong tear off my skin.

"Understood?"

I nod my head in response. That isn't good enough for him. Pulling my ponytail so that my back arches forward, I answer properly, "Yes."

"Yes, what?" His grip tightens as he replies into my ear.

"Yes, husband." My reply won't be taken well, but I can't help but give him a jab to remind him that no matter how much he hates it, we are married.

"You know what to call me." I feel him inhale and exhale. "You were screaming it last night."

I thought hard about what he meant. Replaying what I would rather erase from memory, I say the only other thing I shouted.

"Bozhe moy!"

He groans into my neck as his hands roam freely over my body, tracing the curves of my waist and hips. His hands make their way to my breasts as his hips press against my ass. I feel his cock throbbing in between my ass cheeks, ready to be satisfied as he slowly rocks his hips back and forth while his hands massage my nipples. His entire length covers my crack, with the head just hitting the entrance. My pussy is getting wetter by the second, with the number of sensations happening at once. I've never wanted anything more than for him to be inside of me. Barely able to hold back, a long moan escapes my mouth as I press my body further into his. I want more...no, I need more.

"How bad do you want it?"

"As bad as you want me, too," I breathe.

I am ready for him to take me right here on the cold, hardwood floor, submitting to the turmoil of conflicting emotions, accepting my role beneath him, yet yearning for something more. As I wait for him to continue, he stands, brushing himself off with an air of nonchalance, leaving me breathless on the floor.

"Our flight leaves in an hour." The words feel cruel as they leave his mouth.

Did I say the wrong thing? What just happened? I remain on the floor, the cool wood pressing against my skin, offering an odd semblance of comfort. Is he tired of me already? I should be glad, but instead, I feel empty because I am unwanted. If he is bored with me already, then my days are numbered. How can I get a cold monster to feel something—anything—for me? My life depends on it.

I've endured worse—much worse—and survived. The sound of the shower running in the distance brings me back to reality, the gentle cascade of water a stark contrast to the chaos of the morning. What lies ahead is uncertain, but one thing is clear: I have to navigate this new life, one breath and one moment at a time.

Chapter 20

Adrian

I turn the knob of the shower, watching as the water splashes against the white tiles, steam curling into the air like a serpent ready to embrace me, just like the one tattooed on my leg. The warmth envelops me, as though trying to melt the coldness gnawing inside of me. I stand there, allowing the droplets to cascade over my body, soaking away the remnants of the night before—a night filled with passion, vulnerability, and an ache I fear will consume me.

As the water runs over my skin, I force my mind to dissipate the thoughts of Lana, who surrendered herself to me, her beautiful moaning still echoing in my ears. There is kindness in her—that innate desire to understand, to connect, and it reminds me too keenly of a time I once was the same. Somehow, being inside of her reminds me of the person I was before prison. I am like a wretched little animal, still wary after years of captivity, unable to accept any form of attachment.

I lean my forehead against the cool tile wall, the water washing over me in soothing waves while the past haunts my mind. I can feel the tension coiling in my chest, the way my heart races as I remember:

* * *

"I will wait for you, my love," her soft lips kissed my forehead through the prison bars of my cell.

The fluorescent light in the cell cast a harsh glare that seemed to amplify the starkness of my surroundings. The air around us tightened, each word echoing in the silence of the cell as it was a promise written in stone.

"I'll miss your laugh, your touch, and you," I whispered as our foreheads touched. If only these bars weren't in between us, I'd embrace her.

A tear slipped down her cheek, and she quickly wiped it away, trying to keep a brave facade. "Promise me you'll take care of yourself." She tightened her fingers around mine.

"You are the only thing that will get me to survive here." I forced a smile. "My honeycake."

Our eyes locked, and I saw my entire world reflected in her gaze—the love we had built, the life we dreamed of, and the hope that still flickered in the depths of despair.

* * *

The pain is a ghost that refuses to let me go. I thought love didn't have an expiration date, but I was wrong. I inhale deeply, letting the mint scent of soap fill my lungs; it is a distraction, a desperate attempt to drown out the thoughts that claw at me from the shadows in the back of my mind. But no amount of steam can fog the clarity of my past.

Dear Adrian,

It pains me to tell you this, but it's best you hear it from me. I'm getting married tomorrow. It's not out of love but for survival.

My heart is forever yours,
Your One and Only

Five years. Five years in prison had taught me the lessons of survival, and somewhere down the line, I lost any form of humanity. Love isn't something on my agenda. My goals since my release are to claim my throne and take anyone down who is a threat. Although Lana isn't a threat to my throne but is to my heart. When I got back last night, I found her asleep on my bed, wrapped in my sheets. The sight of her lying there made my cock hard with a desperate longing. I should have killed her when I had the chance. I can't continue to let her distract me from accomplishing what I need to do. As long as she hates me, I am safe from forming any kind of connection. There is something about Lana that moves me. Every touch is a reminder of what had been or what could be again. She's not a reminder of what I've lost but a rush of what I can potentially gain. I clench my fists against the wall. *No.* I fear openness more than I fear pain, and I will never give my heart to a woman again. Not ever.

Letting the water cleanse me is a ritual, a necessity that washes away not only the grime of the past but also the guilt that results from my choices. I step back from the water, wiping the condensation from the tiled wall and staring into the haze of steam that fills the bathroom. I am a man born of darkness; my life is never what it seems. Labeled the prince of the bratva, my life is stained by bloodshed, taking a man's life for the first time at the ripe age of twelve. It was my father's test on whether I had the balls to live up to the bratva lifestyle.

Lana sparks a flicker of humanity, and it terrifies me. The struggle is infinite, a war wages within the very depths of my soul. She is an enemy, and I don't even know if I can trust her. I step out of the shower, shaking off the droplets like a wild animal stepping back into the world. I turn the water off, steam dissipating around me, the clarity of the mirror slowly emerging from the haze. I study my reflection, eyes shadowed, face haunted, yet an undeniable determination etches in my features. Every scar, every line, carved into my skin is a testament that I survived the darkest time of my life.

"Adrian," the soft voice behind the door calls my name.

Abruptly opening the door, I watch Lana eye my naked body up and down. It is the first time she's seen me fully naked, and I can tell it affects her somehow as she holds the sheets close to her body.

"What did you call me?" I reply with an intended tone to set fear back into her.

"Bozhe moy," she rolls her eyes, correcting herself.

Her eyes dart to my cock that just twitched at the sight of her holding back her attitude. I hold back a laugh of amusement. I've violated her and destroyed her world, yet I see no real fear in her eyes when she looks at me. Keeping her in check is to maintain control over her, but damn is it sexy when she throws it back right at me.

"Is there something wrong...wife?" I let the last bit roll off my tongue slowly as I know it ticks her nerves.

"Nothing, bozhe moy," she replies, walking in my direction to get into the bathroom.

My arm shoots out to the side, and I rest my hand on the

frame of the door so that she can't pass. I can feel her breath on my forearm as she exhales through her nose. It is the kind of breathing when someone is left unsatisfied.

"Did you need something?" she questions, refusing to look at me.

"Not at the moment," I reply and then drop my arm so she can pass.

We exchange glances that are as sharp as daggers, our wedding vows hanging in the air like an awkward silence. She is trying her best not to look at me as she goes into the bathroom. Letting her shower in peace, I scan her clothes to pick out something for her to wear. Nothing is appealing at all. Her wardrobe is full of dark and oversized clothing. That needs to change. As I pull out a black T-shirt for myself, I grab my phone to call my sister.

"Adrian? Is everything okay?" Bianca answers on the first ring.

"You worry too much."

"I never know anymore with you." She sighs in frustration. "I barely recognize the person you are."

"Maybe you just didn't really know me to begin with," I snap.

"I miss the person you were before you were locked up in that hellhole. He's still in there somewhere—I know it."

I let out a deep breath as I don't want to disappoint her high hopes that her big brother lost his soul the day he was locked up in that prison cell.

"I need a favor."

"Anything," she replies eagerly.

"Get you and your brother here for breakfast."

"Why?"

"I need you to be a buffer."

"Are you joking?" her voice laced with annoyance.

"Bianca."

With a huff, she answers. "Fine. What's going on anyway?"

"I won't bore you with details."

Just as I end the call, Lana steps out of the bathroom, her silhouette emerging from the steam. She glides into the room, a plush towel wrapped snugly at her chest, another elegantly coiled around her damp hair like a crown.

"I forgot you had a staring habit," she says as she catches me watching her, my gaze lingering as if drawn by an invisible string.

"Until I can trust you not to do anything reckless..." I begin, allowing my voice to trail off, my tone low and playful.

"Oh, yes. Like plot your demise," she quips, her sharp wit shining through her banter until she switches into a menacing tone. "Or kill you."

"I wouldn't grant you that pleasure," I reply. "A viewing for your family will take place in your old home later today as agreed."

Nodding her head, she forces a smile. "It's appreciated."

She picks out a blue and white pinstripe button-down shirt, and her fingers brush the fabric as she holds it up, assessing it as if it is a priceless gem. I'm going to have her entire wardrobe thrown out and replaced with an entirely new one to my liking. As though ignoring me, she lets the towel drop. The fabric brushes against her skin as she slides into my shirt, the hem falling just above her thighs, a scandalous little dress, snug enough to tease but loose enough to incite curiosity.

I can't help but watch, captivated, as she buttons it with a relaxed grace that ignites a fire within me. Each button slips through its hole with a sensual caress, and my breath hitches as I catch a glimpse of her curves once she ties a belt around her waist.

"That's what you're wearing?" I ask when I realize she isn't looking for pants.

"Well, I plan to put on sandals." Her eyes dance with mischief as she looks up at me, a smirk tugging at her lips. "Is that an issue?"

Picking up a pair of nude sandals, she slips them on effortlessly, exuding confidence. She strides toward the door, her hips swaying subtly like a siren's call.

"Where do you think you're going?" I ask, leaning against the wall, my eyes darkening with intrigue.

"Am I supposed to wait for you to direct my every move?" She shoots back, feigning innocence, but the challenge is clear.

"Put on a damn bra and some panties, Lana," I command, an edge of desire lacing my words, recognizing that she is toying with me.

"Oh, right."

I watch her undress, put on undergarments, and re-dress herself, each move done deliberately as though mocking me. Once she is done touching up her face and hair, she stands in front of me.

"Happy now?"

Chapter 21

Lana

The pounding of my heart against my chest feels loud as we silently make our way to the dining room that displays a feast of delicacies waiting to be devoured. My mouth salivates from the smell of Shanezhki topped with Tvorog and the crispy and fluffy Oladi alongside a variety of Blini options of sweet or savory to choose from.

Adrian grabs an apple and takes a bite. I find my mouth salivating again but this time at the sight of him sinking his teeth through the red skin, ripping off a piece and chewing it on one side of his mouth. *What is wrong with me?* As I place a strawberry Blini onto my plate, I hear footsteps enter the room.

"Everything is ready," Ivan states as he walks in, noticing the display of food. "What's the occasion?"

"Not sure what Lana likes," Sergei replies as he shoots me a look. "Had the local baker deliver a few options."

My cheeks flush at the kind thoughtfulness. "I'm not picky."

"Ah, here's the porridge," Ivan says to Sergei. "Care for some?"

Sergei holds himself back as he watches Ivan laugh.

As Ivan walks past me, he leans in. "Porridge is a sensitive topic for him."

Attempting a kind smile, I quickly find my seat at the table. Just when I think this can't get any more uncomfortable, in walks Adrian's sister.

"Adrian," she smiles and kisses her brother on the cheek.

"Make yourself a plate," Adrian motions to the feast.

When she sees me, she holds back a sneer. Her judgmental eyes watch me like a hawk as she takes a plate and pours herself some porridge and a side of fruit.

"Good Morning, Bianca," I smile as she sits across from me.

"Morning," she replies, then turns her attention to her porridge.

Before Adrian can make a comment, in walks his brother with his wife.

"We made it just in time," Gil smiles as they enter. "Looks like you win the bet, darling," he kisses his wife's cheek, then turns to Adrian. "I thought you'd be a widow by morning."

Raya nudges his arm. "Don't be rude." Then turns her attention to me. "I was a bit worried when you both left suddenly."

"It was late," I reply. Directing my next words at Gil, I continue, "Your brother has needs to be fulfilled."

My joke thankfully causes him to burst into laughter. "I think I'm going to like you, Lana."

"Gil," Adrian warns, his voice low and taut, the weight of suppressed tension heavy in the air. I can feel the stirring of something murky, an undercurrent that Adrian clearly doesn't want to acknowledge.

"Relax, Adrian. Just having a little fun," Gil says, the laughter that rolls off his tongue feels sharp, almost mocking. He shoots a sideways glance at Bianca, whose lips curl into a smirk, her eyes glinting with mischief as if reveling in the mounting discomfort.

"This porridge tastes like shit," Bianca spits into a napkin, her expression sour as she pushes the dish away. "Your wife needs cooking lessons." The words land with venom, cutting through the room like a knife.

I stiffen at the comment, my fists clenching in my lap, and a flush creeps up my neck. I can feel their eyes on me, as if they are dissecting every flaw.

"Oslo made it," Adrian replies, his voice barely above a whisper as he picks up his half-eaten apple, its shiny skin reflecting the shifting moods around the table.

"Why is he still here? He can barely warm a cup of milk." Bianca rolls her eyes, her disdain palpable as she leans back in her chair, crossing her arms defensively.

"Adrian is a good man," Gil interjects smoothly, trying to fill the silence with false camaraderie. "Oslo needed a job after getting out of prison." He glances at Adrian while oddly boasting about a great accomplishment.

I shoot a sideways glance at Adrian, who sits there quietly, demeanor unreadable, tension coiling like a spring ready to snap.

Raya transforms the atmosphere with a forced smile, her eyes flitting from one face to another, desperate to shift the mood. "Do you both plan on going on a honeymoon?"

she asks, her tone bright, as though it can dispel the dark cloud looming over the room.

She looks at me expectantly, and against my better judgment, I blurt, "Cyprus." The words hang in the air, and I hold my breath, half-expecting Adrian to lash out, but he merely nods, surprisingly composed.

"Ah, Cyprus is beautiful!" Raya exclaims, genuine excitement lighting her face. "Have you ever been?"

"No, I haven't. My husband—deceased husband," I correct myself, the weight of the room in my throat, "preferred vacationing in Ko Lipe."

Raya turns to Gil, a playful smile dancing on her lips. "You've never taken me to Thailand."

"You name when and we will go," Gil winks at her, his charm effortlessly disarming as he leans back, a self-satisfied grin plastered on his face.

Bianca's throat clears, cutting through the pleasant banter. "Lana, did you come here to be a trophy wife, or do you have some hidden talents aside from picking where to vacation?" As her words drip with condescension, she shoots a look toward Raya.

The subtle exchange between the two gives me a flicker of relief; I'm not the only target of Bianca's scorn.

"Bianca," Adrian interjects sharply, his patience visibly fraying, the muscle in his jaw tightening.

"Oh, come on!" Gil chuckles, crossing his arms casually as if oblivious to the storm brewing. "It's good to break the ice!" His eyes shift back to me, glinting with a mix of curiosity and mischief. "So, any special talents, Lana, aside from managing to stay alive married to my brother?"

I can't help but giggle at his comment. "I'm a very good cook."

"Well, I hope you invite us over for dinner sometime,"

Gil counters, but there is an edge to his voice that suggests a challenge.

"You're not afraid to get poisoned?" Bianca shoots back, her tone rude and dismissive, raising an eyebrow.

"I'll be cooking for the memorial dinner," I reply boldly.

"Memorial dinner?" Bianca questions suspiciously.

I am taking a chance and taking a risk by positioning Adrian into making him do this. He wants to play pretend, then fine. I'll just use it to my advantage.

"Tomorrow marks three days since my family's passing. I plan on having a showing at my old home, followed by a memorial dinner. My mother would have wanted that."

Everyone seems to look at Adrian, who remains eerily stoic. "It will be a small gathering."

"We will be there," Gil replies. "You're a Sokolov now, and we stand together always."

Adrian cuts in, "I'm surprised you are up this early, especially after a night of drinking." Grabbing his apple, he takes another bite. The sound of his teeth cutting through the skin and the crispy crunch of ripping a piece off feels like an unspoken threat.

Gil leans back in his chair with a relaxed demeanor. "There's something I meant to discuss with you last night. I knew being drunk, you wouldn't take me seriously, so here I am. I've been thinking about this a lot lately, and I could use your backing on this, Adrian. You're head of the bratva here in Moscow and on your way to be for all of Russia, but you need to think even bigger! What better way than to lock in power than to also claim the highest position in the country on a more legitimate side?"

Adrian arches his brow. "If you are thinking of getting into politics, just know you're better off joining the priesthood."

"Not just a politician, Adrian. Prime Minister."

Bianca looks between her brothers to try and make sense of what she is listening to.

"You want me to be Prime Minister?" Adrian counters.

"Well, not you. Me." Gil speaks with confidence, but his plan is laughable.

Adrian gives Gil a blank stare. "I think you need to cut back on the drinking, brother." Adrian gets to his feet. "I have a few meetings for the day. Lana, take my black card, get whatever you need."

"Finally learning some pointers from me, big brother," Gil teases, shooting a broad smile at Adrian. "Nothing like spoiling your woman." He pulls Raya in to place a kiss on her forehead.

There seems to be an awkward silence. Adrian clears his throat and replies, "There are a few upcoming events that Lana will need attire for."

"Upcoming events? You barely leave this fortress unless it's to shed blood." Gil pops a grape into his mouth.

"We have dinner this week with the President," Adrian replies nonchalantly.

The room stands still for a moment after hearing this.

Gil stops chewing his food as he looks at Adrian in shock. "How did you manage dinner with the President?"

"Lana's father has a line of connections that have opened a few doors."

My line of vision meets Adrian. He is playing the same game. Forcing a smile, I reply, "Mr. President throws a lavish dinner party for his birthday. My father gets an invite every year."

Gil seems overly excited by this. "Lana rubbing elbows with Mr. President. My brother is one lucky man. I have to admit, I am jealous."

"I'm sure there will be a few notable people who will come to pay their respects tomorrow."

"Sorry for my husband's...eagerness," Raya voices, giving him a look. "When is the dinner?"

"This weekend."

"You're going?" Bianca almost chokes.

"Why is that so surprising?" Adrian asks.

"Because no bratva has ever attended something so..."

"High class?" Gil finishes her thought with a raised brow. "We aren't animals."

"To people like that, we are." Bianca's voice is more like a warning.

Bianca stands abruptly, her chair scraping against the floor, cutting through the tension like a knife. "I'm not partaking in this." The change in her body language is unmistakable. She wants to leave the room in a hurry, and so she does.

"Leave Gil and I to speak," Adrian commands.

"I won't be long, Raya," Gil said. "Meet me at the car."

"I'll walk out with you," Raya smiles at me.

Raya and I leave the dining room and enter the hallway.

"It's always business with them," Raya says. "Something you'll get used to. How did last night go?"

"I took what you said and used it," I smile. "It helped."

"Good," Raya replies, placing her hand around my waist. "I'm here if you need any advice."

Her hand remains there longer than necessary, so I sway my body away casually and change the topic. "So, Gil is looking into politics?"

Raya rolls her eyes and giggles. "Gil is always coming up with ideas, but I have to say this one might actually stick."

"It will be hard gaining public favor with him coming from a bratva family."

"How do you think the most powerful political figures come into power anyway? If they are using the bratva to gain their title, what makes them any different?"

I nod my head. "They live with us or without us, but it's better to stay under the radar."

"Everyone in Moscow knows the Sokolov name, and it's spreading throughout Russia. Now with your connections, staying under the radar is inevitable."

"I'm not sure that's necessarily a good thing." My father might have rubbed elbows with powerful politicians, but it was clear they never saw him as an equal.

Raya shrugs a shoulder. "You'll learn how ambitious this family is. They get what they want, however they need to."

Oh, do I know that very well. "It will be a lot more pressure on everyone's plate."

"I wouldn't mind being lady of the country," she winks.

"Ready, darling?" Gil's voice comes from behind.

Raya glances over her shoulder. "Yes."

"You ladies playing nice?" Gil comes between us, rapping his arms around our waists.

"I always play nice," Raya sways her hips into him.

We reach the front door, and they give their goodbyes. Quickly grabbing a light sweater from the coat rack, I hear Adrian's voice.

"Wife. Let's have a chat."

Chapter 22

Adrian

I walk down the hall with my hands in my pockets while Lana remains still.

"That was slick of you." Removing my hands from my pockets as soon as I stand in front of her, livid. "You really think I'd let your family rest in peace?"

"It would be a bad look if you didn't."

Snatching the hanging chain from her neck, I pull it up toward my chin. Lana tries balancing herself as she grips my forearm with both hands while I slam her back into the wall.

"Don't bullshit me, Lana. I should punish you for that." My face is an inch away from hers.

"You think dinner with the President is good enough? There will be a number of powerful political figures who will come to pay their respects. You will gain a lot more than I will."

She isn't wrong, but it irritates me nonetheless. I

showed her how well I could play her game when I mentioned dinner with the President.

"Your father was a two-faced man who desperately sought applause—it's both tragic and pathetic."

Lana is speechless, but there is anger there. I should have seen it coming, but I'm so focused on instilling fear that I have my guard down. She knees me right in the balls, having me fall to my knees. While still hanging onto the chain, I am now the one looking up at her.

"For someone using all his resources, you have some balls to make a comment like that," Lana says sternly. "So, you can pull on this chain all you want, but respect what I am worth."

Fighting through the pain, I get to my feet and grunt. "I should lock you in the pillory."

"Go ahead," she shoots back.

"Adrian." Sergei stands down the hall, attempting to restrain me from breaking her neck.

Keeping my attention on Lana, I grit, "Stay out of my way today. Don't do anything stupid. You won't like the outcome." I let go of the chain, setting her free.

"Should I make you some tea?"

"I don't drink tea. Now get out of my face."

Lana quickly runs off and doesn't look back.

"Still not playing nice?" Sergei asks.

Ivan comes into view. "Your brother's a prick." He huffs. "What did I miss?"

"Adrian's paranoia is influencing his mood," Sergei replies.

Ivan gives me a confused look. "Who upset the bratva prince now?"

I roll my eyes.

"His dear wife," Sergei smirks.

"Adrian found his match." Ivan gives a hearty laugh.

"You may not trust her, but at least try to be kind," Sergei comments as he observes me.

"How do I trust the woman I stole everything from?" I confess.

"There's only one way to know for sure," Ivan replies. "Test her loyalty as you would for any other bratva."

We make our way into the conversation room where I pace back and forth, my thoughts scattered into a million pieces. There are a lot of loose ends that need to be tightened, but securing loyalty from those closest to me is crucial before finalizing any operations.

With furrowed brows, Sergei asks, "What are you thinking?"

Finally breaking the silence, I reply, "We can arrange for a shipment of weapons that are in high demand right now to be confiscated by the police. Let them arrest us all. If Lana is under police custody, they will surely bring everything they can forward so that she will cave. She will either stay silent and say nothing or side with the law to save herself."

"Trust is a luxury we can't afford," Sergei urges. "That is a risky idea. What if it fails and puts us in a spot we can't get out of? We should focus on the underground railroad."

"Focus will still remain on gaining access to that railroad. In the meantime, I want to know just how committed my wife is to me. Once we know where Lana stands, we take immediate action. If she remains loyal to me, then you burn all evidence down. Police can't make a case without solid evidence."

"And if she doesn't remain loyal?" Sergei questions.

"Then I lock her in that pillory until her body decays."

There is no opposition to the outcome.

"Understood," Ivan replies, the note of loyalty echoing in his voice, and Sergei follows after.

The weight of command settles upon my shoulder as my chest tightens with a storm brewing inside of me. Loyalty, once tested, can become impenetrable armor. And as the shadows deepen in my mind, I prepare myself for the storm that will follow.

Chapter 23

Lana

My feet take me down a hall I haven't seen before, but my fear of the unknown outweighs the fear of the man I am trapped in this house with. The anger in Adrian's voice was chilling to the bone, and the grip on the chain necklace was so tight I can still feel it around my neck. Entering an empty room, I find shelter in the darkness as I sit on the floor with my back pressed against the cool wall, holding my knees close to my chest, my breath shallow and quick as memories flash through my mind like a disjointed film reel. The more I fight against the flooding of my past with every choking gasp, I am transported back to Beau—his imposing figure looming over me, the grip of his hands seeking to constrict rather than caress. Memories of bruises and broken trust flood my senses, a visceral reminder of all I have endured. The way Beau had manipulated me, twisted my own fears against me, was like a shadow that haunted the corners of my mind, whispering lies that I was unworthy of love, that I would always be the victim.

Here I am again, with fear that grips my throat like a vice. I tighten my grip on my knees, trying to find comfort in the smallness of my body. This time, there is no one to blame but myself. I chose this; I agreed to this; I'm vowed to this. Trying to find the strength within me as I shut my eyes tightly, willing the visions away and focusing instead on the sound of my own breath, the tears fall silently, tracing the lines of worry etched across my face.

"There you are."

I gasp at the sound of Adrian's voice and tremble as he walks into the dark room uninvited. He stands in front of me so that all I can see are his legs until his hand comes into view. Refusing to take it, I remain still.

"Don't make me be mean."

His lack of an apology hangs in the air, heavy and laden with sincerity. It isn't much, but it is more than Beau ever said. I give him my hand and allow him to help me up but avoid eye contact.

"I don't like talking about personal affairs around my brother," Adrian says.

I look up at him with visible anger. "That's not a good enough reason to be an asshole."

The words leave my mouth, and when I see Adrian's eyes widen, I know he will reach for the chain. I brace myself for the pull, but nothing happens. Adrian raises his hand and releases the chain necklace, dangling it in front of me. My hands touch my neck only to find it bare. It must have fallen off, and I didn't realize it. The sheer panic rises as my heart races, and my mouth goes dry.

"Beau, I'm sorry. I..."

The realization of what I just said causes me to fall

back. Adrian steps forward, closing the gap between us as we lean against the wall.

The silence is thick, but his response is immediate. "What did you just call me?"

"I-I didn't mean it," I reply.

Adrian drops the chain onto the floor and grabs my hip. His free hand gently wraps around my neck. I can feel my heart thumping against his thumb as it gently caresses my neck. Our noses touch for a brief moment before he glides it across my cheekbone and to my ear.

"What is my name?" His whisper is a deep drum in my ear.

"Adrian," I breathe.

His hand tightens around my neck just a bit as though it is a reminder. "Bozhe moy!"

Lifting his head so that I can see his face. "It looks like I need to do better at making you forget your old life."

His mouth crashes onto mine, taking me by surprise. His kiss is anything but soft and sweet. Filled with hunger and possession, his tongue strokes mine, making my body flare with heat as they dance. My hands unbuckle his belt and push his pants down before gliding over his obliques, making their way to his broad shoulders. Adrian uses both his hands to rip open the front of my dress, causing all the buttons to fly across the room. Lifting me into the air, Adrian slams my back to the wall, pinning me against it with his body. I find myself losing control, instinctively wrapping my legs around his waist, allowing him to sink further into me. He pulls his upper body away for a brief moment. Using his hips to keep me in place, as his one hand reaches to unhook my bra, he watches my breasts break free. My pussy is leaking as my body aches for him. I wrap my arm around his neck and pull him back in so our mouths collide once again. Effortlessly, he rips apart my underwear. His big hands cup the back of my thighs, and he lifts me higher and pulls them apart so that he can sit me on top of his erection.

I feel the head of his cock at my entrance, aching to get inside despite how wet I'm getting. Adrian's hands move to my ass for a tight squeeze before gliding them up my hips, along my torso, stopping at my breast for a squeeze. He breaks from our kiss so that his mouth locks onto one of my breasts, causing me to pant and moan. Moving my hip further into his body makes him bite down on my nipple.

"Bozhe moy," blurts out of my mouth.

I feel his mouth curve up into a smile in victory then glides his teeth against my skin until my nipple pops out of his mouth. Those thick hands make their way to my back and up toward my shoulders, gripping them tightly as he pulls down. I shout from the pain of his cock forcefully entering me. Adrian lets out a deep growl. The walls of my pussy tightly suffocate his cock as it throbs from excitement.

"Are you still thinking of him?"

Caught in a haze, I shake my head. Who is he even talking about? My mind and body are fully consumed by him.

"You still want him?" he mocks, thrusting deep inside of me.

Lost in a euphoric moment, I can barely hear anything he is saying. Despite the hatred I feel for what he's done, I suddenly want him badly. My body betrays me yet again, craving the touch of this monster. "I never wanted him," I confess.

"Beg to cum on my cock," he demands.

The words leave his mouth, and it takes my brain a

moment to process them. "Fuck this pussy until you bust inside me. Fill me up."

Relentless. Savage. Out of control. I hold onto him tightly as he pounds inside of me until I am on the edge. But right when my eyes are about to roll back, Adrian pulls away from me. My legs are wobbling as I try to stand straight. I watch his erection glisten as he removes his shirt and steps out of his pants before lying on the ground.

"You want me to fill your pussy up, then come do the work."

I hover over him, but those tangled emotions of hate and lust mess with my head. Turning around, I position myself so that my back faces him and slide his cock back inside of me. His toes curl once my pussy suffocates his cock again, and now I wear a victorious smile. Moving my hips forward and back, I get right back into it. Adrian's hands grip my hips, pushing down so that when I swing my hips backward, my clit glides across his shaft as I thrust back forward. I toss my head back as waves of pleasure flutter through my veins. Forward. Back. Forward. Back. Allowing myself to give in to Adrian's odd sense of remorse, my body erupts, and I freeze for a moment as my orgasm rips through me. His hands still grip my hips gently, moving them forward and back until I am ready to finish him off.

My eyes catch the chain necklace on the floor. He has banished me from the shackles, and I want to make sure he knows how much that means to me. While still inside of me, I drop my upper body forward and grab onto his ankles. Before Adrian can ask what I'm doing, my hips bounce up and down, fucking him. My breasts lay on his knees, and I tightly grip his ankles for balance. I give him a full view of his cock entering and exiting my pussy. He doesn't need to make a sound, his body tenses under me, letting me know he's the one surrendering now. Without a pause, I keep my pace going until his hands grip me tightly, and he thrusts his hips upward. The feel of hot cum shoots inside of me, plastering the walls, and the sound of Adrian's growl ripping through the room feels like I entered a realm not on earth.

I wait for his body to relax as he comes down from his high before crawling off him. Sitting beside him, we look at one another as though looking at a blank canvas.

Then reality snaps in, and Adrian sits up. "The viewing for your family will be tomorrow. One day only. No ceremony. Are you good with that?"

I nod my head. He gets to his feet and walks over to where the chain is bunched up on the floor. Picking it up, he stares at the chain as though dissecting it. Finally, he looks up and straight at me. With his eyes, he gestures for me to come forward.

What a fool I am to think he will break me free of his shackles. One day he will, though; I can feel it. There's a barrier I need to break through, just like Raya said the night of our wedding. All I need to do is keep submitting. Getting on my hands and knees, I crawl to him. When I reach him, I remain on my knees, sitting upward. He wraps the chain around my neck and loops the heart through the other end. This time, the chain feels lighter.

Chapter 24

Adrian

I stand to the side of the viewing room, the air thick with somber whispers and the scent of fresh flowers. The ornate chandeliers above cast a dim light over the gathering, illuminating the sorrow etched on many faces, but none more striking than Lana's. She floats between clusters of Russia's most elite political figures, her laughter cutting through the solemn atmosphere, a stark contrast to the bratvas here who remain cautious of everyone around them.

I know Lana's family held power through the oligarchs here, and it's now made clear how differently we have grown up. Even wearing a tailored black suit, it is visible which is the criminal and which has an aura of decorum and prestige. I can almost hear the murmurs of the guests dissecting us behind polite smiles. They know who I am, what I am, and I can smell the fear behind each hello.

Lana is effortlessly charming, her smile wide and

inviting as she engages with an oligarch named Bren, who has just returned from a high-profile meeting in Brussels. The way she tosses her hair back and laughs lightly at something he says makes my chest tighten. I shift my stance, crossing my arms in a subconscious gesture of protection as I watch them interact. The senator leans closer to Lana, his movement conspiratorial, as they discuss some legislative maneuver. Even in grief, politics pour from his lips like wine at a lavish banquet. That's enough for me to begin walking toward them.

"That's a strategic advantage you've got there, Lana. The media will eat it up," Bren remarks, a smirk playing on his lips. I catch the glint in the politician's eye that gives away what Bren's true intentions are.

"It's all about positioning, isn't it?" Lana replies, her back to me, unaware that I'm approaching.

She isn't wrong; it is all about positioning. Yesterday hasn't stopped playing in my mind. Under the innocent exterior, she is a vixen. I wrap my arm around her waist and pull her into me, nestling my mouth to her ear as though playful, while my line of vision is directed to Bren, ensuring he knows Lana is mine. He receives the message very clearly, and he uncomfortably adjusts his tie.

"Adrian Sokolov," Bren says my name as though speaking me into existence with fear in his eyes. "I thought you were in prison serving life."

A sly smile crosses my face as I stand up straight. "People forget I made a deal with the devil. No one can put me away for good."

"I didn't realize Lana was acquainted with you."

"It's more than an acquaintance. We are married." I hold up Lana's hand along with mine to show the gold wedding bands that wrap around our fingers.

Lana's body tenses. "With Beau passing, Adrian has been very generous to me."

"I'm sure of that," he glances between Lana and me. "Lana, my deepest condolences. Truly. Your father was such a good businessman," Bren says. "If you ever need anything, please don't hesitate. I owe it to your father."

Lana nods to him with a smile. "Thank you, Bren."

As we watch him walk away, I whisper into her ear, "Are you embarrassed by me, wife?"

She turns to face me. "Are you jealous?"

"Why wasn't he aware you were married?"

"Why is that important?"

"Looks like you might have some history there."

She huffs in frustration as she lowers her voice. "And if there is?"

"If I haven't already made it clear, you are mine, Lana. Whether you like it or not, Russia views you as my property, and I don't like trespassers."

"What, you plan on killing him, too?"

I enjoy her sharp tongue and desperately want it wrapped around my cock.

"I will erase any trace or memory of any man who has laid eyes on you, touched you, or even had provocative thoughts of you."

My thoughts were interrupted by a woman with perfectly coiffed hair and a tailored red outfit moving in our direction. "Lana, darling!" she coos, her voice dripping with affection as she hugs Lana in a too-tight embrace. "My condolences, darling. But I see you have jumped right to it. You married so quickly."

"Madame Aleksandra Morozova," Lana smiles, rolling off her title with ease.

I watch the Prime Minister's wife, who commands

attention without demanding it, speak to Lana as though she is a niece to her. Ivan and Sergei linger in the background, waiting for me to give some command, but I wave them away. It will be too obvious if the Prime Minister's wife goes missing after paying respects to a woman married to a Bratva king. No one here is to be touched.

"My poor child, my heart aches for you." Sasha brings her attention to me. "Despite the sadness of today, your name is on every tongue in this room." Her hand reaches out toward me, and her fingers lightly grab the lapel of my suit jacket. "Lana darling, he is much better than Beau." Her eyes glaze over my muscles wrapped under my suit as though she wants to lick the skin off my body.

I can feel the anger radiating off Lana as she allows Sasha to fawn over me. To women like her, I am a fantasy they wish to live. They can't handle the danger or lifestyle of a bratva man, but they get off on imagining it.

"Adrian, I hope you will continue the Volkov tradition." Sasha glances at Lana with a sly smirk. "We all look forward to the Serpentine Ball."

I place my hand onto hers, which is still holding my lapel. "Whatever you wish." Bringing her hand to my lips, I give it a light kiss.

"I will be waiting on my invite then," Sasha smiles proudly and walks away.

With a smirk, I look to Lana, who is no longer standing beside me. When I lock eyes with Ivan, he nods his head in the direction she went. Walking out of the room through the crowd, I find Lana heading toward the exit. There is fury in her stride, which causes me to smirk. Following closely behind her, she pushes through the door, and a brisk breeze hits my face. Quickly grabbing her arm, I pull her to the side and push her against the building. To my surprise, there are streaks of tears running down her face.

Quickly wiping them away, she sniffles as she straightens her posture. "What?"

Closing the gap between us just enough to be an inch away, I lock eyes with her, then slowly study her face. These aren't tears for her family.

"Jealous?" I question, carrying a smirk of cockiness.

Lana lightly growls in frustration. "You could only wish."

"Well, you are upset. So if it isn't another woman touching me, then what is it?"

"My parents and husband are dead," she clears her throat and looks away. "Is that not a reason to cry?"

She is lying.

"I wasn't aware your father was behind the lavish Serpentine Ball."

It seems to have hit a nerve as Lana rolls her eyes. "You think any of those people would invite him to one of their own parties? He blindly invited them to a party, for which they had no idea who was throwing it. My mother would entice their wives and mistresses enough to want to attend by making it a night of pure indulging. That's how my father got in with them."

"I assume your husband Beau did a fair share of indulging."

Her body tenses as she deeply inhales, confirming my assumption.

"Did you not do the same?" I ask.

She lets out a laugh. "Like I would have the same courtesy of doing so even if I wanted."

As much as I want to hear that she hates seeing

someone touch me, I think it would be best to make this into a learning experience.

"Why is that?"

My question seems to have surprised her. "You know as well as I do that Beau controlled everything I did."

Stepping closer to her. "You don't need to have a choice when you can make people do exactly what you want without saying a word."

She furrows her brows. "No man would even think to look in my direction."

"It's not because you aren't attractive, Lana—if you haven't noticed, all eyes were on you in there."

"Out of respect for my father, they would never step out of line."

"You mean out of fear," I correct her. "Did you notice the fear in Bren's eyes when I approached you versus the excitement in Sasha's eyes as she fawned over me?"

Lana shifts on her feet, looking to get around me, but I lock her in place with my gaze. Even with my hands in my pocket, I have control over her.

"Fear is what made Bren walk away from us earlier. Respect is what you showed Sasha, even when she didn't take her actions against you into consideration. Let that sink in."

Stepping to the side, I reach for the door handle but stop when Lana shoots back with, "Sasha never respected me. I know that. Each time my husband lay with her, she proved it."

I let my arm fall to my side as I turn to face her. "So why allow her to mistreat you?"

"She is the Prime Minister's wife."

"That's not a reason."

"I don't hold the same influence as she does."

"Maybe not with Beau, but now you are married to me." The words shoot out of my mouth in anger. "You now have more influence than she ever will. It's up to you to let her know that."

"I don't want to be feared; I want to be respected. That will always hold more value."

"And you are confident you're respected in there?" I nod my head toward the building.

"Of course. They are here to pay their respects after all."

Letting out a laugh, I reach into my pocket and toss her small pieces of paper. "Here are all the women who gave me their numbers without asking. Some even have a set day and time they demand to be seen."

The handful of small torn pieces of paper disperse into the air in front of her face as she stands in shock. With the look of defeat, I can see her mind racing with confusion as though her entire life is a lie.

"If they are so bold to do this behind my back, then there's no changing their ways."

Now I am the one frustrated. Grabbing her face, I bring it close to mine. "You make them. As the woman carrying my name, do not let anyone believe they are above you. There's an unspoken fear in the Sokolov name, and you better make sure you hold up to it."

"You want me to chop off their fingers?" she sarcastically suggests.

"Fingers, hand, arm. Do what you want to make a point, and when you do it, make sure everyone receives the message loud and clear."

"Oh, yes. Let's set up a stage by the caskets and really put on some entertainment."

"Don't tempt me with a good time."

The door to the building opens and out walks Sergei, who sees me grabbing Lana's face.

"Sergei, bring Bren to me."

Lana's eyes widened as she struggles to get out of my grip. "Leave him alone."

Letting her face go, I open the door to the building. "Let me show you how fear trumps respect."

Chapter 25

Lana

I am sure more than ever now that Adrian has no regard for how things are done. Do I want to be walking around smiling and socializing with these two-faced elites? At least with bratvas, it is understood what they are, and they don't hide from it. Ivan leads us to the basement of the funeral home, which is where they cremate the deceased. The smell is rancid but doesn't seem to bother Adrian or Ivan. The walls are lined with metal tables and cold storage.

"I don't know what you are trying to prove here," I comment. "Jealousy is an ugly look on you, Adrian."

"You're about to see just how ugly I can get."

Footsteps coming down the stairs echo through the room.

"Where are we going?" I hear a voice.

"Shut up and keep walking," another voice replies.

One last attempt to change Adrian's mind, I almost beg.

"I know what you're doing. You're trying to instill power over everyone by making them absolutely terrified of you."

"Done well for me so far," he replies unapologetically. "How do you think I was able to get Beau to turn on your father?"

The comment is a punch to my gut. "Beau was only loyal to himself."

"Things would have gone differently if Beau were terrified of going against him." Adrian gave a smug smile. "I was surprised he wanted to keep you alive."

"I was his wife—why wouldn't he want me alive?"

A light chuckle breaks from his mouth. How ironic how much I replayed his mouth on my body yesterday, and now I want to smack it off his face.

Soon enough, the two voices come into view. Bren walks in looking nervous as Sergei follows behind him. His body remains tense when he sees Adrian and Ivan in the room. However, once we make eye contact, his shoulders seem to relax, while my breath is caught in my throat. Sergei pushes him toward us.

"Bren," Adrian smiles as though they are good friends. "Word is buzzing around that you plan to run for the Federal Assembly."

Bren nods. "That is the plan. The Federal Council specifically."

"It would be a shame if there were a hole in that plan."

Bren looks in my direction. "What is going on here?"

"My wife here," Adrian gestures toward me, "thinks very highly of you."

"She's a respectable woman herself." Lifting his chin up in admiration.

"She is something, isn't she?" Adrian walks closer to Bren, pacing his way like a caged wolf waiting for their prey to drop their guard. "I know her support will get you a few votes."

"I can only hope so." Bren straightens his posture. "Although I'm sure you're looking to make a proposal. You can buy others but not me. My name won't be tainted by you."

"Your name is just a whisper in the wind." Adrian's posture radiates an undeniable authority. "There are plenty of others who have a better shot at winning."

"You seem to forget which side of the law you fall on. It will only take me a phone call to the police, and you'll be back in that prison cell."

"You wouldn't put your good friend, Lana, here in that position, would you?"

I watch Bren's body stiffen. "Leave her out of this," he speaks cautiously.

"Do you not care for her well-being?" Adrian threatens.

"Of course I do." Beads of sweat form on Bren's forehead.

"Then it's agreed. I'll make sure you win your seat on the Assembly, and you will remove the President and push for my brother Gil to take his place."

A nervous laugh escapes his mouth. "Are you crazy? That will be political suicide for me."

"What if I told you there are other seats that will be taken who will back the same?"

"No one would want a bratva in that position."

"I'm not worried about that."

"What's to say I'd keep my end of the bargain?"

"Think of your wife and children. Their livelihood and safety depend on it." Every word out of Adrian's mouth drips with a deep-seated conviction.

"Don't involve them in this. I don't take threats kindly."

"It's not a threat, Bren. It's a promise."

"Why me? It's a lose-lose."

Adrian turns to me, shifting the room's focus in my direction. This conversation is making my stomach turn.

"Lana doesn't feel as though she is worthy. I think it would set a good example. Since you admire and respect her so much. This shouldn't be a difficult choice."

Bren remains silent. Adrian reaches into his jacket and pulls out his gun from his holster, then places it on the table beside them.

"Although if Lana isn't with us, then we can pretend this conversation never took place. My offer is off the table, and we continue with the lives we know best."

There's an unspoken challenge, and the air around me feels heavy. Bren's hands tremble at the sight of the weapon.

"You want me to kill her?"

"Or yourself," Adrian suggests as the alternative. "The choice is yours."

A heavy silence envelopes the room, punctuated only by the sound of Bren's shallow breaths. As he takes the gun, a mixture of fear and desperation twists his features.

"Bren, you don't have to do this. It's just a sick game." My voice trembles.

"Is it?" Adrian challenges, his voice dripping with menace.

There is a fleeting moment of recognition in Bren's eye —a moment where he understands the power dynamic at play.

"I'm so sorry, Lana," Bren swallows hard right before he pulls the trigger.

Time seems to slow as I gasp, waiting for the bullet to hit. It sounds off, causing me to instinctively shut my eyes. But I feel nothing. Slowly opening my eyes, I see Adrain holding Bren's arm upward so that the bullet hits the ceiling instead of me. Silence reigns thick with tension as Bren's face contorts in pure panic.

"You are right, Bren," Adrian says. "It was a lose-lose for you."

An arm comes around Bren's neck. I watch a hand take a large knife and cut it across Bren's flesh like swiping it through water. Bren drops onto the table, blood spilling everywhere. My brain is still registering what happened while Ivan and Sergei step right in to remove the body.

"This just proves you're a psychopath," I spit out.

"Is that the thank you I get for saving your life?"

My body trembles. "Saving my life!?"

"Fear is a powerful tool," he walks toward me with ease. "People like Bren—men of ambition—are driven not by admiration but by fear of losing everything." His voice deepens with an ominous murmur that entwines with my unease. "Imagine having the power to control someone's fate simply by exploiting their fear."

"This wasn't exploiting, Adrian. You took his life just to prove a point." I punch his stomach. When he doesn't flinch, it upsets me more.

"Does that make you feel better? Go ahead, do it again."

Two more blows and he barely moves, so I begin pushing. "He has a wife and children."

Adrian allows me to keep assaulting him. "Bren didn't seem to care about you when he pulled that trigger."

Breathing heavily from tiring myself out, my head falls onto his chest in surrender. "I hate you."

"I'm okay with that."

Looking up to see his face, there is no remorse. "How are you not afraid to get tossed back in prison?"

"I didn't get here by being afraid. I got here by making others afraid."

"We'll get a cleaning crew down here," Sergei says.

Ivan shuts the cremation chamber door. "I'll watch him cook."

Adrian lifts my chin with his finger. "You are going back up there like nothing happened. Put that smile on your face and act like you never saw Bren here."

"When he's reported missing, this will be his last known place seen."

"And who would say anything?"

Even the most elite wouldn't dare go against Adrian. If I didn't know it by now, then I surely know it now; I'm married to the most lethal man in Russia.

Chapter 26

Adrian

Lana does exactly what she's told. I continue to watch her from afar while I converse with others. Her words ring in my mind like a carousel. *You are a psychopath.* I always find glory in hearing people call me all types of things, yet with Lana, she seems as though she would have expected better from me. Maybe if we met before I went away, before I was tainted with darkness that has permanently stained my soul. Call me a killer or a heartless monster. I'm a villain by the devil's law, and I am not ashamed of it.

Gil approaches me after finishing a conversation with two oligarchs who have agreed to push a border policy that will work in my favor.

"For someone so anti-social, you have been the chatty one today."

"When it comes down to business, little brother, I have no choice," I remind him. "What do you think you will be doing all day as Prime Minister?"

A smile crosses his face. "So you have thought about it. Finally, we can agree on something."

"I haven't been convinced just yet, but there is something you can do to help me decide."

"Ask and you shall receive."

"See that woman there?" I nod in the direction of Madame Sasha Morozov. "She's the Prime Minister's wife. I think she's quite lonely."

Gil observes Sasha, who is laughing with a group of women. "I can change that. Too easy a task. What purpose does it serve?"

"That project I spoke to you about yesterday."

"The railroad running from Western Europe through Asia." Gil nods his head.

"Word is that the Prime Ministers of every country the railroad runs through will help funnel money to purchase products men like us supply. Make friends with Sasha—we need an in."

Gil smiles with joy. "I'm thankful you let me have all the fun."

"What kind of big brother would I be if I didn't."

"Are my eyes deceiving me?" my father steps in cautiously. "My two sons are speaking, and neither has reached for their gun."

"Adrian and I are beginning to see eye to eye," Gil replies.

"Good." My father places one hand on my shoulder and one on Gil's. "Your power falls on the strength of your bond. You both need each other."

"Oh, my favorite men." My mother glides over to us. "Adrian, I must say, Lana has impressive connections. I hear the President is due to arrive."

"You should thank her then," I reply, knowing my mother will never do such a thing.

"We are family, Adrian," she goes on with her excuse. "There is no need to thank family for doing what is expected."

"Interesting. You seem to require the same from Raya."

The three of them look at me with a puzzled face. Sure, Raya comes from the same lifestyle, but the only thing she has brought to this family is a headache.

My mother rubs Gil's back as though comforting him. "Don't mind your brother, Gil. I know Adrian and Bianca tend to gang up on you."

"He's not wrong, mother," Gil replies, looking at me. "Raya hasn't upheld her promises."

"Don't bash your wife," my mother begins.

"Family meeting?" Bianca sneaks up from behind.

"Just the usual banter," I comment. "The Petrovi throw an annual ball each year. We should continue that tradition."

"That's wise, my son." My father gives my mother, Gil, and Bianca a look, causing them to disperse.

We begin walking away from the crowd and toward a more secluded area.

"Gil has been persistent about running for Prime Minister." I sharply inhale in frustration.

"It's not the worst idea," my father replies.

"I won't allow it."

"Adrian, you must reconsider. Look at the doors Lana has opened up for us. We need to take advantage."

"It doesn't work like that. Lana's father made sure to keep his connections under the radar. It would be smart to keep it that way. This private showing proves it. If this were an open showing, none of these people would be here."

My father urges on. "I've been talking to a few federal assembly members. They can be easily swayed."

His gray eyes used to hold so much power. It was something I always admired. Now they look old and weak, unlike mine, which hold a coldness that no one can mistake as a threat.

"You don't call the shots anymore," I remind him. "I said no."

"It's foolish."

I stop in my tracks and turn to face him. "What's foolish is letting someone like Gil hold a position he can't handle. What happens when he fucks it up?" My voice gets a little louder. "I went to prison for you and ended up getting sentenced to life. I won't make that sacrifice again."

He stiffens at my words. "You were only supposed to get a few months."

"Well, that didn't happen, did it?" I turn around and begin walking back in the direction we came in. "Lana is making dinner tonight. If you want to be there, then you are welcome."

"Adrian," I hear Lana's voice approach me. "I need to get started on the memorial dinner. I've already made my rounds to everyone."

"Sergei will take you back. I'll make sure everything here is wrapped up."

* * *

The next two hours are slow, and I've never been so happy to go home. Making my way to the dining room, the smell of a freshly cooked meal hits my nostrils, beckoning me to come and have a taste. The dining room, usually understated, is transformed into a warm haven. Lanterns cast a soft glow while the long mahogany wood table is dressed with a crisp, white tablecloth that elegantly drapes to the floor. Golden candles are lit in clusters—their soft light reflecting off polished silverware that gleams like stars against the deep blue plates. Each one is carefully arranged, and each dish is already decorated with an Olivier salad that seems to have the perfect amount of mayonnaise.

The door to the kitchen swings open, and in walks Lana, now out of her black attire from earlier and in a more comfortable outfit. Still in black, she wears a simple T-shirt that stops right under her belly button and a wide leg trouser, so effortless and relaxed, just as she appears to be now. Carrying a pot holding a plant full of bright red berries, she places it at the center of the table.

Tossing my jacket onto a chair, I loosen my tie and unbutton my shirt from top to mid chest. It is a casual yet mindless act, but as I watch Lana, she doesn't seem to look away. It is a moment of unspoken truth, yet I'm not sure what she is confessing to. A citrusy smell mixed with florals begins to invade the air in the room.

"What is that smell?" I question. "Oranges and, is that jasmine?"

Lana looks to the plant. "I took it from my father's garden. It was his favorite plant. No one was allowed to touch it but him."

"I didn't take you as the sentimental type."

She shrugs. "It's easier to be disconnected, but I figured it would be a nice touch to this memorial dinner." Her big brown eyes soften as she speaks.

"Everyone should be here soon," I say.

Lana smiles. "Good. I made beef stroganoff."

It is another favorite dish of mine, yet I can't bring

myself to say that. The less she knows about me the better. No strings attached here.

"I'm starving and it smells delicious in here!" Gil shouts from outside the room.

Making my way to her, I cup her face in my hand, and my thumb caresses her cheek. Both Lana and I back away from one another as my family piles into the room.

"Interrupting something?" Gil asks with a sly smile.

"Everyone can have a seat," Lana smiles.

I sit at the head of the table and watch everyone take their seats. Lana takes a bottle of wine from the table and begins to uncork it as everyone begins to eat.

"Lana, this tastes amazing," Raya voices.

"I see your mother taught you well," my mother adds. "Bianca barely knows where the kitchen is located."

This is how my mother operates, now that she knows how worthy Lana is to fueling our power, she will do and say anything to uplift her even at the cost of her own daughter. My eyes go to Bianca who holds her tongue. Lana begins pouring everyone a glass of wine, and we all wait until she gets to her own cup so that we can do a toast.

"Thank you all for being here," she smiles. "It means a lot to know that you see me as one of you."

"We are happy to have you in our family, Lana," my father holds up his cup. "To you and your passed loved ones. May their memory forever reign."

"Cheers," Lana holds up her cup, and we all do the same.

As we drink from our cups, Lana continues to speak. "I learn something everyday being here, and I take each lesson to heart." She looks around the room. "Today's lesson was the power of fear." Placing her cup back onto the table, she sits in her seat just watching us.

The eerie gesture makes the room fall silent.

"Lana," Raya speaks up to fill the uncomfortable void. "What a beautiful centerpiece."

She reaches to touch it but halts when Lana replies, "Thank you. It's a Volchya Yagoda."

Then I realize she never drank from her cup nor tasted what is on her plate. This is a rare plant to have if living in Moscow, and I have never seen one up close before. Everything in this plant is poison: the berries, the leaves, the stem...hell, one drop of its juice causes severe skin irritation.

"Lana," her name growls out of my mouth in a low and deep threat.

"What's going on?" Bianca asks nervously.

"Poison." My father gets to his feet.

Everyone begins to panic as Lana watches and enjoys the show. She's bluffing, but she is good at it. If any of us had the plant in our system, the signs would show. No one appears dizzy or nauseous. My mother and sister are screaming while Raya is hyperventilating. Gil doesn't know what to do, and my father is livid. I do my best to hide a smirk.

"Everyone out!" I demand.

"Adrian! We need to go to the hospital!" Bianca screeches.

"No one is dying." I gulp down the rest of my cup.

Ivan and Sergei bust through the kitchen door to see what the commotion was. "Get everyone out."

I pace the room until the only ones left were Lana and myself. Clapping my hands, I applaud my wife. "Good acting."

"Who says I was?" she shoots back.

"You want to prove you have the balls, you get points for creativity, but I'm still not scared of you."

"You should be."

Chapter 27

Lana

Was it a stupid idea? At the moment, I still think it's clever. I want to convey the message that I'm not afraid without having to actually harm anyone.

"I could have poisoned you and your family. I still can."

Adrian laughs as though it's comic relief, and I watch him walk over to the plant and pluck a stem off that has five berries attached with three leaves. He is clearly a madman to have touched the plant with his bare fingers. I don't know how he does it, how he manages to instill more fear into me than I already have of him.

"You should have just poisoned us, Lana." He unbuttons the remainder of his shirt with his free hand, leaving his chest and torso exposed. Adrian stalks toward me, and I quickly get to my feet, my eyes glued to the piece of the plant he is holding in his other hand. "Now that I know you have access to this, you'll never see it again, and I'll have eyes on you like a hawk. What little freedom I gave you is now gone."

I gulp at his threat, knowing he's not bluffing. Regret is slowly creeping up. He holds up the plant as he stands face to face with me. There is no doubt I will be the one who will be suffering tonight. Reaching out, he drags the plant along my collarbone, causing a tingling sensation.

"In prison, we would trade the leaves from plants like this as if they were gold." Adrian's vision is on the plant and where he lightly drags it across my skin. "If you had means to pay off a guard, they would bring you hot water. Ingesting the plant itself is poisonous, but if you boil the leaves, it becomes a hallucinogenic tea." It was like he was being transported back to that dark place. "You needed just the right amount to get you through the day. Too much would fuck you up."

My skin tingles wherever he teasingly drags the plant across my skin, the sensation amplified by the plant's leaves. His eyes linger on my lips as the silence stretches between us, thick and heavy. Adrian is analyzing me as though he wants to break through the walls built between us but won't allow himself to. I watch as he plucks a berry off, the top letting out just a little juice. I hold my breath as I watch his next move.

"I'm sorry," I blurt out from nowhere. "For whatever happened to you in there."

My apology seems to snap him out of this trance. "It's not your fault."

"I know," my breath hitches, "but I can see the torment through your eyes."

I want to push him away, to maintain the distance we always keep. But something is clouding my judgment, heightening my senses, making me acutely aware of his nearness. I can smell his cologne, feel the heat radiating from his body, making my skin prickle and my nipples tighten beneath my cotton shirt.

"You know what I like about you, Lana," Adrian steps even closer. "No matter how frightened you are of me, you're still here."

Taking the berry, he lightly coats my bottom lip with its juice. Immediately, my skin becomes irritated. My tongue pokes out and wipes across my bottom lip, and the gesture lights up Adrian's eyes, squeezing the berry in between his fingers then tossing the rest of the plant onto the floor. Adrian glides his finger along my neck, transferring the juice onto my neck. I am beginning to get lightheaded but also feel like my body is starting to float. Licking the juice off my neck, his tongue, warm and moist, touches my skin, igniting heat under my flesh.

It is infuriating how arrogant this man is, and yet, there is something about him that makes my pulse quicken.

Adrian speaks against my skin, "You're trembling." His thumb slides down my jaw.

My eyes flutter shut at his touch. I haven't noticed I am trembling because this time it's not from fear. It is something else—something primal. My lips slightly part, my breath coming in short low gasps.

Adrian's other hand moves to my waist, pulling me closer. "What's wrong, Lana?" he asks, his voice a husky whisper. "Are you scared?"

I open my eyes, meeting his gaze. His gray eyes are dark, intense, and for a moment, I see something in them I've never seen before—desire. It's making my heart pound harder in my chest, and my body is responding to his in a way I can't control.

"I'm not scared of you," my voice barely above a whisper.

His lips reach my jawline, and I feel them curve into a smirk. He enjoys tormenting me, and I think I enjoy it just as much.

"Are you feeling it?" he asks, his hand sliding down to my hip, pulling me even closer.

I catch my breath as his body presses against mine. The feel of the hardness of his muscles and the heat of his skin sinks into me. My mind is foggy, my thoughts scattered, but my body knows exactly what it wants. I tilt my head back, parting my lips at his invitation.

Adrian's eyes darken further, and I can sense his control slipping. He leans in, his lips brushing mine in a teasing kiss. I let a soft moan slip out of my mouth as my hands come up to clutch his shoulders. The moan gets muffled as his lips enclose onto me. The kiss deepens, our lips moving in sync, our tongues tangling in a dance that is both familiar and utterly foreign.

The plant creates more power—enhancing every sensation, every touch, every sound. My body is on fire as I feel every inch of him, every breath, every heartbeat. It's overwhelming, intoxicating, and I want more. Then out of nowhere, his body pulls away from me.

"Adrian." Ivan seems as though he has been attempting to gain his attention without success.

"What is it?"

"The police are here."

"For what?" Adrian asks.

Ivan nods his head to me. "For her."

A wave of shock hits me but quickly replacing it is the realization that this was planned when Adrian's look of desire vanishes into a cold stare.

Two officers enter the room. "Lana Sokolov, we need you to come down to the station."

"Take her," Adrian states unfazed.

Chapter 28

Lana

The room is dimly lit, the walls bare cement, and a single flickering fluorescent light swings slowly overhead, casting shadows that dance across the stark space. A table separates me from the two detectives, Tal and Havi. We sit at a narrow metallic table in the center of the room, which feels oppressively cold and clinical. I attempt to appear composed yet defiant, my hands clasped tightly against the icy metal and my back straight, but the residual effects of my high pull at the edges of my focus, making my thoughts flutter like the shadows on the walls.

"May I call you, Lana?" the heavyset officer asks politely, leaning forward, resting his forearms on the table, his gaze steady.

"You may call me Mrs. Sokolov," I reply sternly, though there's a slight slur to my words, a lingering haze clouding my clarity.

The younger detective, who has a casual air about him, reclines in his chair with his arms crossed, tilting his head as he studies me. His fingers drum against his small bicep in a steady rhythm, contrasting with the chaos in my mind.

"Do you understand why you are here?" he asks, his eyes narrowing slightly.

"Well, it isn't because you asked for a private showing." The sarcasm slips out before I can reel it in, but at least it distracts me from the electric buzz dancing behind my eyes and the way my heart seems to race in time with the flickering light above.

With a mix of authority and impatience, the heavyset officer holds his composure. "We have evidence linking your husband to some serious crimes. You can help yourself by giving us something useful."

As I lean forward, unyieldingly with a smirk on my face, I say, "And what information could I possibly offer you that would be useful?"

"When was the last time you saw Bren Olkov?"

My eye twitches, a delayed reaction to the haze of smoke still swirling in my mind. "He was at my family's viewing today."

They share a look. "And who was the last person you saw him with?"

"My focus that day was on my parents and late husband," I reply, words feeling slippery, like they might slide away if I don't grab hold tightly.

"You mean the people your husband killed?" the heavyset officer hits back, the accusation slicing through my fog like a knife.

"My husband didn't kill anyone—at least not that I have seen." The room spins slightly, but I steady myself, focusing on the sound of my own heartbeat.

"You are protecting a monster, Lana," the younger

officer replies crisply, his voice echoing unnervingly in my ears.

"Mrs. Sokolov," I correct him, the need to assert my identity battling the weight of my confusion.

"Adrian is a criminal who uses violence, fear, and intimidation. We know he killed your husband and parents."

I feel laughter bubbling up unexpectedly, a defense mechanism against the barrage of accusations clouding my thoughts. "If you had enough evidence, you would have already locked him away." My voice remains steady, chin held high, though inside, fear churns like a storm. "Instead, you are using me as leverage."

The heavyset officer begins to tap his pen against his notepad, the rhythm resonating with the racing thoughts in my head, like a beat I can't escape. I clench my fists tightly, nails digging into my skin, grounding me amid the rising tide of uncertainty. The interrogation room feels dimmer, time stretching as I struggle to keep my focus.

He leans forward, his voice dangerously low. "Imagine losing everything—the life you built, all gone because you chose loyalty over truth."

"You don't know the truth. If you did, I wouldn't be here. My family died at the hands of their enemy, and I needed to make sure I wasn't next. That is the truth, and it's your job to find the killers." I gulp, hoping I am convincing and that the beads of sweat on my forehead aren't too noticeable. I fight to maintain composure as their threats hang in the air.

The younger officer begins taking another approach as the room remains charged with tension. Opening the manila folder in front of him, he takes a deep breath, trying to maintain control before pulling out several gruesome photographs, their edges worn slightly from handling. One by one, he places them in front of me to view, each photograph worse than the last.

With a cold, menacing tone that doesn't match his innocent appearance, he begins. "These are from a recent crime scene. Look closely, Mrs. Sokolov. Your husband is responsible for this."

Quickly glancing at photos of a mutilated man has me holding back a gag. Despite avoiding looking at the photographs as best I can, both officers don't hold back.

"We received a call about a suspicious pile of debris out in the Ryn Desert that would link us to an ongoing investigation."

The younger officer gets to his feet and hovers over me, placing one hand on the metal table and the other on my chair. "What we found was a bloated corpse, marinating in the hot desert sun. Do you know what happens to a body that has been sandblasted?"

The heavyset officer shakes his head as if trying to erase the image from his mind. My eyes begin to water from the horror as my stomach knots in disgust.

"Take a look," he places a photograph in front of me that makes me wince. "The body is exposed to relentless wind and sand until it erodes, bones stripped bare, and flesh disappearing."

My breathing hitches, the grotesque imagery imprinted in my mind.

"This is the man you lie with every night," the heavyset officer chimes in with a judgmental look, placing another photograph in front of me.

"He sliced open this man from sternum to his pelvic bone."

A tear slips down my face. "He's been with me every day. He couldn't have."

"Every single day?" the heavyset officer questions. "Not once did he disappear for a while?"

"We know his pattern, Mrs. Sokolov: choosing a victim to be his drug mule. Having him gutted, packing him full of product, stitching him up with fishing line, and then transporting him out to the desert to rot.

"You act as though my husband is the only drug lord walking this earth." Another tear slips down my cheek.

The younger office leans in closer, his mouth close to my face, then places another photograph for me to see. "His neck was slit open."

The heavyset officer in a calmer voice adds, "Do you know who that is?" When I don't answer, he tells me anyway, "Igor Petrov—your uncle."

I draw in a sharp breath from the tension but remain silent. They exchange another glance, showing a hint of frustration creeping in.

"You understand by not complying, you are an accomplice?" The younger man stands straight rolling up his sleeves.

"I've done nothing wrong," I insist.

Slamming his palm on the table, visibly agitated, the younger officer shouts, "You're not leaving this room until you cooperate!"

"Then you might as well get comfortable," I shoot back.

The tension is palpable, silence hanging heavy as I lock eyes with them, a fierce fire igniting in my gaze. If I help them and get Adrian convicted, then I will be hunted like an animal. My odds of survival are higher protecting him then trusting these musors.

The door opens, and another officer enters, signaling it's time to leave. "Fun is over. She isn't under arrest, and I have an attorney here to make sure she leaves right now."

The two officers sneer at me. "Until next time."

Chapter 29

Adrian

"**A**drian, what is going on?" My father's concern is understandable.

"I didn't want Lana to be embarrassed when the police came." This is my excuse for them clearing the room.

"Why was she taken?" my mother asks.

"I'm sending Sanders to the station to find out. For now, everyone go home, lie low, and I will call you in the morning."

"Adrian," Bianca's voice is shaky, "They won't take you away again, will they?"

"I will never let that happen again," I assure her then shoot a look to my father.

"Let us know what happens," Gil replies, helping me guide them out of the house.

This is bad timing. After seeing my family out, I go find Ivan and Sergei.

"This could have waited a few days." I enter the room and see them sitting and waiting for me.

"That was the plan," Ivan replies with confusion. "Nothing was set in motion yet."

My demeanor is calm on the surface, but under my skin is an odd sense of guilt. "What did Sanders say?" I ask, hoping my attorney gets to the station in time to know what is going on.

I sit on the leather couch with a bottle of vodka, gulping down each cup like a shot as Ivan plays with his pocket knife and Sergei smokes a cigarette.

"She was in the interrogation room when he got there," Sergei replies. "They found her uncle's body."

"The slimeball. How?"

"I made sure he couldn't be detected," Ivan chimes in. "The only way they would have a clue is if they were tipped off."

"You still need proof it was him," Sergei says before inhaling a puff.

"What if it's the person threatening you?" Ivan asks. "Whoever it is, they are a ghost. I couldn't find anything."

"It's been silent so far," I reply.

"So far," Sergei repeats. "We should focus on finding who sent that Queen of Spades to your father. Just because it's silent doesn't mean they aren't plotting."

"My concern right now is Lana."

Sergei taps his cigarette on the ashtray to rid of the ashes. "She's been there long enough to know she hasn't given them anything useful. If she did, they would have released her already and you'd be back in prison."

There is a sense of relief that sets in but doesn't overshadow the mistrust lingering beneath the surface.

"Or she could be playing both sides," Ivan adds, playing devil's advocate as he cleans his knife with a cloth.

Ivan validating any ounce of doubt puts a pit in my stomach.

"One thing is for sure, no one trusts a musor," Sergei challenges. "Whether she is protecting herself or you, that kind of loyalty, whether it comes from fear or respect, is what keeps the bratva world alive. If you go down, what makes her think she won't be their next target?"

Ivan weighs in. "She could be agreeing to being their mole until she knows she's safe to flee."

A thick oppressive silence falls over the room as the scale between loyalty and safety weighs its options, my gaze flicks between them both as they are waiting for my verdict. "I need to know if she's playing a game or actually can be trusted."

I pour vodka, filling my cup halfway and gulping it down as the storm inside of me brews. This isn't what I had planned. The weight of contemplation is heavy on my shoulders. Trust is a fragile thing, but sometimes, you have to take risks, especially when the stakes are high.

The sound of footsteps approaching the room gets louder.

"I'm back," Lana softly speaks, her voice thick with exhaustion, betraying the weariness that clings to her like a heavy fog.

A wave of relief washes over me at her return, though it churns my stomach. I realize I'm getting too soft with her; the vodka in my glass warms me, dulling my sharper instincts.

"We were just discussing how to dismember you if you threw me under the bus," I remark, half-joking, but my voice carries a jagged edge. I can feel the warm buzz of the alcohol, swirling in my system, making me wonder if I should keep sipping or rein it in.

There's a newfound fear in her eyes that I can't ignore. Ivan and Sergei remain seated, their expressions unreadable, as I rise from my chair, the movement feeling heavier than usual.

With a snap of my fingers, I point to the ground, commanding her, "Come here."

Cautiously, she steps closer, her eyes flitting nervously between the three of us. The moment she catches sight of Ivan holding his blade, I see her body tense up, the earlier bravado faltering under pressure.

"Thank you," I say, lifting my cup in a mock toast before taking a sip. "Usually, women cave under pressure." The statement hangs thick in the air, my breath slightly alcohol-laced, as I battle the fog clouding my mind.

Confused, she asks, "How do you know that I didn't tell them anything?"

Her question reveals the uncertainty gnawing at her despite the façade of strength she tries to maintain. The vodka buzz washes over me, and in that moment, I wonder if she can sense the intoxication that softens my resolve or if it just makes me appear more unpredictable.

"Did you?"

"They showed me photos of my uncle."

"My condolences."

Lana inhales as though calming her nerves. "I know our families weren't allies, but there was no reason to take my uncle's life. I'm married to you. His life didn't depend on mine."

"A bratva always seeks vengeance. I wasn't going to just let him go."

"You can't just get rid of everyone in my life."

Getting to my feet, I stand tall. "I can, and now you know that without doubt, I will."

"You will never be satisfied, will you?"

"Do you loathe me yet?"

She looks at me with a blank expression as though I said the most ridiculous thing. "Loathing you means that you win, and I won't let that happen."

"I've been too kind then."

She scoffs. "There's nothing you can do or say to make my life worse than what it was before you."

There is such defiance in her tone that I know she isn't bluffing. How bad could her life have possibly been?

"I find that hard to believe, princess."

She makes her way to me slowly, swinging her hips side to side.

"You want to humiliate me by making me wear a leash and walk me around like a fucking dog. I'll take that any day compared to my husband who would beat me daily for just being in his presence." She stops in front of me and takes the drink out of my hand. "You take my body whenever you please, even when it is against my will. I'll take that any day compared to my mother letting me starve because I wasn't thin enough." She gulps down the vodka in one shot. "You need to be in complete control of me to satisfy your ego. I'll take that any day compared to my father who sold my virginity to gain access to the one border everyone ached to have." She placed the cup down on the table. "It's impossible for me to loathe you. You've shown me the most love I've ever had in my life."

I stand looking at her, speechless. Her eyes water, turning red holding back from crying as she waits for me to dismiss her. I don't have words to muster together even though I can't take my eyes off her. There is a silence that speaks this odd sense of unity against the hostility that simmers in the very air we breathe.

"Go to bed, it's been a long day," I wave her off.

The room remains silent until she leaves.

"She might just be as fucked up as you are." Sergei seems as surprised as I am.

"That's not a good thing." I pick up the bottle of vodka and take a chug.

Ivan makes a point. "For starters, she has nothing to lose. That can work for you or against you."

Sergei weighs in. "She already told you that you've shown her more love than her own flesh in blood. Imagine the loyalty that she would give you if you showed her some affection. A scorned woman is dangerous, but a woman in love is fierce, ready to move mountains and face any storm to ensure her lover is safe and happy."

"I will not fake my emotions," I reply. Call me whatever name under the sun, but I will never toy with someone's heart.

"You want to secure your throne?" Sergei challenges.

I take a deep breath and then exhale. "Book us a trip to Cyprus."

"You hate Cyprus," Ivan comments.

I shoot Sergei a look. "My wife said Cyprus for our honeymoon, and she's never been. I can show her a good time."

"Which one of us will come with you?" Ivan asks.

"It's my honeymoon, I don't plan on leaving the hotel."

"Looking to knock her up?" Sergei asks cautiously.

"Do I need to?" I shoot back. "I thought all I needed to do was make her feel loved."

With a shrug, he hits me back with, "Having a kid could

help. That way, if anything happens to her, the inheritance stays in the family through the child."

It's not a bad idea, but I can't picture myself as a father, and I don't want to.

"All the more reason you should have at least one person as back up," Ivan suggests. "The goal is to get you both back in one piece."

"If they don't kill each other first," Sergei smirks.

"You didn't hear them the other night," Ivan shoots back.

Chapter 30

Lana

I sit on the bed with my heart pounding through my chest like it is going to burst free. The pictures are glued to my memory. My uncle and father were close, and I knew he would come to avenge his death, but I didn't think he would be so careless. Adrian showed him no mercy, and if he doesn't trust me, then I will face the same fate or even worse. Changing into a yellow satin short night cami, I nestle myself into the bed. When the door opens, I sit up, clinging to the sheets. Adrian walks in with a calmness that I haven't seen in him before.

"It wasn't personal," he admits as he removes his shirt.

"Which part?"

"I don't know why you were called in, Lana. That wasn't me. I'm not trying to get rid of you."

"And my uncle? Did he need to die so cruelly?"

"I can't apologize for who I am."

"So, what are you apologizing for?"

"That you had to see it. Still, you didn't give me away.

That won't go overlooked." He removes his pants and tosses them on a nearby chair. "Let me make it up to you."

I'm not sure what he has in mind, but I am curious how the devil makes amends for his sins. "Don't think fucking my brains out will do the trick."

He flashes a smile that makes my heart thump.

"I was thinking of something less selfish of me." He walks toward the bed. "Pack your bag. We leave for Cyprus in the morning."

Staring at him in disbelief, I am speechless. We are locked in a stare-off—both of us grateful yet still skeptical. Swinging my legs off the bed, I hop off and walk toward the closet that holds my weekend bag. As I pull the large weekender bag out, it slips out of my hand and lands on the floor, with items falling out. I scramble to pick them up as my cheeks flush at my lack of poise.

"Lana?"

Looking up, my jaw drops open at what he is holding.

"I'm insulted." Adrian walks over to me, laughing.

Quickly getting to my feet, my cheeks red as a rose, I try to snatch it from his hands.

"I didn't know what to do with it," is the only response I can think of.

"You don't know how to use a dildo?" he sniffs it. "Smells like you. I think you know how to use it just fine."

I gulp. "I meant when I moved my things here. I haven't used it."

"I didn't ask if you have."

"I'm sorry."

A mischievous smirk on his face sends the heat in my cheeks through the rest of my body. "You've shown me I can trust you, but do you trust me?"

"I'm guessing you want to test that."

The air between us thickens, charged with unspoken desires and old resentments. Adrian walks to me, tossing the dildo onto the chair. Standing face to face, his hands grab my silk cami and pull it up over my head. Holding each end, he twirls it so that when he places it on my face, it covers my eyes like a blindfold, preventing me from seeing, but I can sense the heat of his gaze on my body. Taking a finger, he glides it along my skin as he walks behind me. I can feel him moving around me, the soft footsteps and the faint scent of his cologne teasing my senses. He is a force, a storm waiting to break, and I am the eye, calm and willing to be swept away.

His hands make their way to my hips, pulling me toward his hard frame. Those thick hands slide up my body, then cup my breasts so firm and possessive. The feel of his mouth trails down my neck, teeth grazing my skin, sending shivers down my spine, and causing my body to arch involuntarily. The silence between us is a barrier that only heightens the tension. Adrian's hands are everywhere, exploring, claiming, his touch both tender and ruthless. His lips move lower, brushing against the sensitive skin of my collarbone. I gasp, my senses overwhelmed, my thoughts a blur.

My legs fly up as he picks me up and lays me on the bed. He steps away, and I am then left in the silence. A moment later, I feel a light touch on my inner thigh, followed by a soft, warm breath. Adrian's lips brush against my sensitive skin, sending a jolt of pleasure through my body. He kisses and nibbles his way up my thigh, his five o'clock shadow tickling my skin, until he reaches the edge of my lace panties.

"I can feel how much you want this," he whispers, his voice hoarse with desire.

I can barely speak, my breath coming in short gasps. "Yes," I manage in a mere whisper.

With slow, deliberate movements, he slides my panties down my legs, exposing me completely. The cool air teases my exposed flesh, and I feel a surge of vulnerability and excitement.

"Let's see how much pleasure you can take," Adrian says, his voice filling with dark promise.

The room is silent for a moment before I hear a humming sound. I gasp as something is placed on my inner thigh, teasing me with its vibrations. My body instinctively reacts to the sensation, causing me to sharply inhale. He continues to tease me, moving the vibrator closer to my pussy, but never quite touching where I crave it most.

"I've barely touched you and you're already wet," he says, his voice laced with amusement.

He positions the vibrator at my entrance, and with a gentle push, he slides it inside me, filling me with a pleasurable sensation. He adjusts the settings, and the vibrator hums to life, sending waves of pleasure through my body. I can't hold back from letting out a moan, my hips moving involuntarily as I surrender to the sensations while I fist the sheets around me.

As the vibrator continues its rhythmic dance, I feel a smooth surface caressing my thighs, the sensation contrasting with the vibrations inside me. Then, with a swift removal, a sharp sting hits my ass cheeks. I gasp, my body tensing at the sudden pain, but it quickly transforms into a searing heat that spreads through me. I moan, a mix of pleasure and pain coursing through my veins.

"You enjoy a good spanking," Adrian praises, his voice a soothing balm.

"You enjoy giving it more," I reply.

"Do you trust me, Lana?"

The feel of something being wrapped around my ankles has me slightly concerned. I am unable to close my legs shut due to something preventing me from doing so. He begins alternating between spanking me with what I imagine is a paddle and using the vibrator. Each strike of the paddle is followed by a wave of pleasure. Spank. Vibration. Spank. Vibration. It's building pleasure, my body arching and begging for his touch.

Just when I think I'm going to peak over the edge, everything just stops. I lie there unable to see as Adrian leaves my body throbbing with unfulfilled desire. When his fingers return to my skin along my inner thighs, my body is brought back to life. Then I feel something on my clit, his fingers sliding through my wetness, eliciting a moan from my lips. My body aches for release, desire building to an almost unbearable intensity. He removes his touch from me again.

"Adrian." I'm panting from an overload of sensation. "Please. I want you to fill my insides with your cum."

My heart pounds as I realize he doesn't have to tell me to beg; he's making me do it of my own will. I have never fully submitted to him, but in this moment, I want nothing more than to give myself over to his desires.

"Do you understand what you're surrendering to?"

"You win," my voice trembling. "My body is yours."

The sound of his ring hits something metal, which catches me off guard at first, but when my body gets flipped over onto my stomach, my thoughts go into a blur. The material around my ankles has tightened, making me realize what he was using on me. I've seen these at my father's freak off parties. Straps are tied around the each ankle, and in between is a metal bar. That's why I am unable to shut my legs, and instantly I feel myself getting wetter knowing this.

Lifting the bar up, my knees are bent toward my back as Adrian puts his weight on the bar and pushes my knees apart with his own. Propping my hips upward so he has the perfect view, I wait for him to claim me. We both grunt when Adrian thrusts his hips into me, using all his force. The room echoes with skin to skin slapping mixed with moaning and cries of pleasure. My legs get tossed in different positions as Adrian moves the bar to his liking. The silk cami being used as a blindfold slides off my face from the impact of his body hitting mine, and at some point, he has my head pushed down into the mattress. My hands fist the sheets, holding on for dear life. The room feels alive and exhilarating, making me fucking delirious. Forgetting everything about myself while I let this man run me like a wild river surging against rocky banks threatening to over- flow, each thrust igniting a blaze that consumes every thought and feeling. The world around me fades away, and all that matters is reaching my climax.

I feel the weight on my head lighten as Adrian removes his hand and grips my waist as though it would steady me. His movements are powerful and savage, yet there is a connection between our bodies, so much so that we both climax at the very same time.

"Bozhe moy! I love you." The words spill out like a confession I had buried for too long. My brain didn't even process it before my mouth said it.

Where did that come from? The weight of my confes- sion lingers in the air as Adrian lets go of the bar. Silently, he removes the restraints on my ankles, and I slowly turn onto my back. Adrian's gaze shifts, and an unreadable expression crosses his face while we both look at one another, unsure where to go from here.

"I didn't mean that," I choke out.

His mouth slightly opens as though he wants to say something, but nothing comes out. Instead, Adrian just turns on his side and goes to sleep. Staring up at the ceiling, I fight this odd feeling of attachment that wasn't there before, and it scares me. Carefully sliding off the bed, I walk over to my closet and push my way to the back where I have placed my favorite novels. Pulling out one of my favorites, I jump into bed and read until I fall asleep.

Chapter 31

Adrian

We arrive at the airport and board the plane. Neither Lana nor I speaks a word. Lana takes a seat as far away from me as she can, and neither of us bothers to converse. After last night, Lana's behavior is different. It's not surprising considering she let the words *I love you* slip out of her mouth. I ignored it, figuring it was said out of the heated moment, but now I'm thinking somewhere deep inside her, it was a confession. I want to avoid any kind of emotional attachment on my end, but if I want her to fall for me, like Sergei suggested should happen to ensure her never-ending loyalty, I need to put on the charm. The issue I am facing is our destination.

I've been to Cyprus enough times to be able to picture it in my head. The sun-drenched coastline shines with golden sand and sparkling turquoise waters, fringed by lush green hills. The rhythmic lapping of waves against the shore creates a soothing melody while seagulls squawk overhead. The air is infused with the salty scent of the sea, mingling with the aromas of grilled halloumi and souvlaki wafting from nearby restaurants. The burst of flavors that invade your tongue with every meal pairs with refreshing local wines. The warm sand slips between your fingers, creating a comforting embrace that relaxes you. The number of times I mentally escaped my prison cell to envision being on this island with the woman I loved with all of my being was the only thing that had kept me sane until I received that letter that shattered my heart.

I get out of my seat and begin pacing around the private plane. Lana looks up from her book to speculate what I'm doing. The invasion of memories floods my head, and I am doing my best not to react. I am well over my past lover, but it's the betrayal that will always rip my heart open again and again. Taking a deep breath to anchor my inner turmoil as the silent battle rages within me, I decide to finally break the silence.

"What are you reading?" I question Lana.

"Anna Karenina," Lana replies timidly.

I didn't take her for a Leo Tolstoy fan. Walking over to her, I sit in the seat opposite her with my arm propped on the armrest as I slightly slouch back.

"Isn't that about infidelity?" I arch my brow. How ironic given my mental state at the moment.

Lana shifts in her seat and shuts the book using her pointer finger as a bookmark. "It's about a woman in a loveless marriage who finds what her husband lacks in another man."

"Is that not adultery to you?"

She bows her head in thought then looks up again. "If you think I will do the same," she lightly shakes her head, "I won't."

"That's not what I asked you." Even I can sense the growing irritation in my voice.

"Is it by default adultery? Yes. But a marriage with no emotional aspect is just a contract between two people to stay together until death do them part."

"Like ours," I conclude.

"I don't see it quite that way."

The tightening of my fist doesn't seem to scare her, although I know she notices. "Then how do you see it, Lana?"

"Anna is a victim—a product and consequence of the society she lived in during an era that was not kind or understanding to women in her position."

"What do you consider yourself if not a victim in our arrangement?" I lean forward and reach toward her neck. My finger traces along the chain necklace around her neck, reminding her who she married.

"This is a mutual agreement," she replies, "You gave me a choice."

Her chest rises and falls in long breaths, the neckline of her dress scooped low enough to showcase her breasts, which are perfectly positioned under the blue sundress. My pointer finger and thumb wrap around the chain that hangs from the necklace in an attempt to distract myself from wanting to rip her dress off.

"Mr. and Mrs. Sokolov, please fasten your seatbelts. We are about to land," the stewardess announces.

I let go of the chain and sit back in my seat. Anna Karenina was my grandmother's favorite Tolstoy book, and when she passed, I would read it each year before I went to prison. It is a complex novel. Each time I read it, I see it through a new perspective. Anna's lover always seems to dance around the concept of love, almost afraid to give in. I find myself relating to his uncertainty.

I know no peace and cannot give you any...and I do not see any possibility ahead either for me or for you. I see the possibility of despair, of unhappiness...or I see the possibility of happiness.

Chapter 32

Lana

Adrian remains silent after our brief exchange over my book. His eyes watch me as though waiting for my betrayal. After my third glance up from my book, I close it shut and place it into my bag, which rests beside me. Adrian doesn't move or even flinch.

"You're staring," I comment.

Silence. I attempt to look out the window to cut whatever tension is continuing to build up, but when my eyes go back to Adrian, I am still being met with an odd stare. It isn't his usual cold look, and I'm not sure what to expect.

"Why didn't you have children with Beau?"

The question takes me by surprise. "I guess it just wasn't in the cards for us."

Adrian is silent for a moment. "Are you able to?"

"No doctor has told me I can't." I know he isn't asking out of curiosity. A man like Adrian has a purpose in every question and action he makes. "Is this your way of asking if I want children?"

"This is my way of saying I don't want any."

"I guess that settles it then."

His brows furrow. "It doesn't bother you?"

"Does it bother you that it doesn't bother me?" I shoot back.

"If you did end up with a child, then what?"

"That's more of a question I would ask you. If you don't want kids, Adrian, and I end up pregnant, where does that leave us?"

"You would abort it if that's what I want?"

Agreeingly, I reply, "If that's what you want."

This doesn't seem to please him at all. What does he want from me? I never think about having children, and I am grateful Beau didn't knock me up. God knows I would have terminated that child in a heartbeat.

"I've never met a woman who didn't want children or who was even open to abortion."

"You've said it yourself, Adrian. I am your property, so it doesn't really matter what I think or want, does it?"

"Have you aborted a child before?"

I was hoping the conversation wouldn't come to this. An uncomfortableness itches under my skin.

"Once." It is better to confess the truth. "I'm not proud of it, but it was necessary."

"Necessary?"

"My life depended on it."

"Were you upset?"

"Naturally."

"So, if your life didn't depend on it, you would have had the baby."

"Yes."

Adrian continues to look at me, questions swirling around him.

"When you say your life depended on it. Was it because of a medical issue or because he wouldn't marry you?"

Sharply inhaling at how keen Adrian is without me having to say much, my body language confirms it is the latter. He leans forward, placing his hand on the chain necklace and then lightly tugging it toward him.

"He was a fool." His nose brushes against mine, causing my senses to awaken.

"I was the fool," I confess. "For letting me be fooled."

He inhales me. "Just say the word, and I will take his life."

My cheeks flush, and I hold back a smile. "Is this your way of flirting?"

"Is it too direct?" He lingers near my face, causing my breath to quicken.

"It's just right."

His lips brush against me. "I know what I have in front of me."

His assurance seems genuine, and it gives me relief that my words last night didn't scare him away. We land and find a white Porsche 911 Targa 4S with red interior waiting for us. The top is down as we ride out of the private airport and toward our hotel. The wind whips through my hair, making it impossible to see. Once I manage to hold enough of it out of my face, we arrive at our destination. The sun hangs low in the sky as we approach the opulent Anassa Hotel, an absolute luxury nestled against the sparkling Mediterranean Sea.

One of the hotel valets opens my door, and I step out of the Porsche while admiring the hotel. Adrian wastes no time getting out of the car and walking toward the door, stopping short as he waits for me to catch up. As we walk through the grand entrance, you are immediately enveloped by a sense of elegance and tranquility. The air is fragrant with a mix of blooming bougainvillea and the faint scent of sea salt from the nearby ocean. The staff welcomes us with warm smiles and cool glasses of champagne. They all seem blissfully unaware of the life we are escaping from. We each take one glass of champagne, then walk toward the front desk.

The spacious lobby features high vaulted ceilings adorned with intricate woodwork and soft, ambient lighting that casts a warm glow. Luxurious, plush sofas invite you to sit, while marble floors glisten beneath your feet. As I glance around, my eyes are drawn to the stunning artwork that decorates the walls, each piece telling a story of the region's rich history. Outside, the serene view of the turquoise sea is visible through expansive glass doors, tempting me to explore the beach just steps away. The gentle sound of water trickling from artistic fountains creates a soothing background melody. It seems like the perfect balance of luxury and nature, inviting us to unwind and indulge in the beauty of the island. A friendly receptionist, dressed in chic attire, greets us with a welcoming smile, immediately making me feel at home.

"Mr. Sokolov," the receptionist greets Adrian. "We are preparing the Adonis Aphrodite Suite for you. If you would like to sit under our pergolas and sip a refresher while you wait. I have a table for two at the Pelagos—our shaded al fresco taverna. It overlooks the pool, gardens, and the sea. I highly recommend ordering the Rosé."

"Thank you," I reply while Adrian just places his arm around my waist, leading me in the direction of the restaurant.

The middle-aged woman looks at me with a tight smile.

"You must stay here often."

"Why don't you grab us a table," Adrian says to me. "I'll be there in a minute."

"Is everything okay?"

"I need to make a quick call."

Simply nodding my head, I head toward the restaurant. Immediately, I am seated at a charming wooden table, nestled in lush greenery and blooming flowers from the vibrant garden while overlooking the sea in the distance. The pergolas cast dappled shadows, creating a serene atmosphere as the sun filters through. The gentle breeze carries the scent of fresh herbs from the kitchen, mingling with the salty air. A soft murmur of conversation and the clinking of cutlery fill the space, enhancing the tranquil setting. This intimate blend of nature and elegance offers a peaceful escape where time seems to slow down, completely relaxing my body and setting my mind free of worry.

A young waiter places two perfectly chilled glasses of wine on the table. "Paphos Rosé," he says, "It's one of our local wines. Whenever you are ready, I will take your order," he says, handing me a menu.

"Will do," I reply, allowing him to place the menu in front of me.

I sip my chilled wine, savoring the crispness as I glance at the menu filled with Mediterranean delights.

"Lana?" a familiar voice calls out my name.

Chapter 33

Adrian

With a nod of her head, I watch Lana head toward the taverna. Her sundress wraps around her body, moving to the sway of her hips.

"I want the Andromeda house." I turn to address the receptionist.

Quickly scrambling to make the change, she nods in confirmation.

Stepping into this hotel makes my stomach turn, but it is the best hotel on the island, and if I want to bring on the romance, this is the place to do it.

Needing a minute to myself, I run my hand through my hair as though that will wipe away this unsettling feeling that is beginning to swirl around me like a storm. Pulling out my phone, I see missed calls from Ivan, Sergei, and my brother Gil. My first callback is supposed to be Ivan, but my phone rings and it's Gil calling again.

"Gil," I answer, "I told you not to bother me for a few days."

"I know. I'm sorry. It's important, though." His voice is anxious.

"What is it?"

"I got into my car today, and on the steering wheel, there was a Queen of Spades."

I went silent. "Check your cameras."

"Nothing," Gil replies. "It's like a ghost, Adrian. You need to come back."

"We just got here."

"I should have canceled your reservation." Gil huffs in frustration. "You're gallivanting around while someone is fucking with us."

"You'll be fine. I'll call Ivan and tell him to send more security to your place. For now, don't leave the house."

"Says the man who gets to hide away in a beautiful abyss while I'm caged in my house. How do you like the hotel?"

"Decent enough."

"Enjoy it. I had to hear Raya bitch about giving our weekend away, and now she's going to go full psycho when I tell her we have to stay in the house."

"I'm sure you'll make it up to her."

"I plan to dick her down all weekend, maybe she'll forget."

"Good luck with that one."

I hang up the phone and dial Ivan.

"Boss."

"Gil got a Queen of Spades. Send some extra security to his place."

"Will do."

"Do we have any leads on that?"

"Sergei is meeting with a family out in Petersburg. Apparently, they have been getting the same threat."

Hanging up the phone with Ivan, my next call is to Sergei.

"Boss."

"How's Petersburg?"

"Colder than where you are. There's a family out here—the Vaksmans—that claims they have been receiving these for a few months, but nothing's come of it."

"Keep looking for something."

Closing my eyes and inhaling the light air around me, I open them once my mind settles from spiraling. As I head toward the restaurant, I attempt to clear my mind. For now, my focus is going to be on Lana and making her fall for me.

"Mr. Sokolov," the hostess welcomes me. "Your wife is waiting for you. Follow me."

I follow, and when Lana comes into view, I see two people standing by the table. The host extends her arm in Lana's direction, leaving me to continue solo. As I approach the table, I can see Lana is uncomfortable.

When we make eye contact, she jumps to her feet. "My love," she smiles, pulling me into her and locking her lips to mine.

I play along as I hold her body pressed against mine, kissing her for longer than needed. Something tells me that Lana is trying to impress them. When we pull away, I pretend to ignore the two people in front of us until Lana clears her throat.

"Adrian, this is Alicia and Maksim," she introduces with a subtle enthusiasm. "Adrian is my husband."

"Husband," Alicia says, seeming surprised but joyful.

"Nice to meet you, Adrian." Maksim holds out his hand to me, and I shake it. He winces at my grip.

"How do you know my wife?"

Alicia and Maksim both glance at one another.

"College," Alica says while Maksim states, "High school."

Lana speaks up, "We were all really good friends."

She keeps her composure, but I'm all too familiar with betrayal of the heart.

"Ah, this is the one you caught with your best friend," I say with confidence, although I don't know if it is true.

By the look of the three of them uncomfortably looking away, I know I hit the nail on its head. This also must be the same man who caused Lana to get an abortion. Now I'm really looking to have some fun.

"What brings you to Cyprus?" I ask as though I care.

"We live here," Alicia smiles, thankful to change the topic.

"You always did say you love it here," Lana replies.

"How are your parents, Lana?" Maksim now ignores me entirely. "They were always so welcoming."

There is a hitch in her voice, "They passed not too long ago."

"I'm so sorry," he replies.

"Oh Lana," Alicia steps forward wanting to give a hug but then stops and steps back. "I'm so sorry to hear."

"I killed them," I admit.

Both Alicia and Maksim awkwardly smile, debating if I am mentally stable.

"You shouldn't disrespect her parents with a bad joke," Maksim says.

"Who said I'm joking?"

They both look to Lana for some kind of under-standing.

"My husband is Adrian Sokolov."

Blood drains from Maksim's face as he realizes I'm not joking.

Alicia's eyes widen. "I thought you were taken to prison."

"And now I'm here." I smile proudly.

"Mommy! Mommy!" Two kids run toward Alicia and Maksim.

They quickly pick up their children and hold them safely away from me. I watch Lana as her posture shifts and her body tenses.

The little girl with blond curls asks, "Mommy, it's the girl from the photo."

Alicia blushes and in a low voice confirms, "Yes, sweetie." She looks at Lana. "I keep a photograph of the three of us by the bed. It's from college graduation."

Lana says nothing, just stares at them. By the looks of it, the oldest child is at least 7 years old. They don't know about Beau or keep tabs on Lana.

"Is that a souvenir for you?"

My question confuses her. "What do you mean?"

"You keep a photo of the three of you by your bed. Is that your trophy? Does it feed your ego every time you look at it when you lie beside him?"

"Okay, that's enough," Maksim's voice is stern but very low.

He gulps when my eyes divert to him. "I'd call you an idiot, but letting Lana go was the best thing that could happen for me."

I wave over one of the waiters who sprints toward us. "Mr. Sokolov, how can I help you?"

"You can escort these people out."

"You can't do that," Maksim says.

But he is proven wrong when, without a word, look, or

snap of a finger, two security guards come to remove them from the premises.

"Apologies, Mr. Sokolov. They will be permanently banned."

"Good."

As I turn toward Lana, who finally snaps out of her haze with eyes full of tears, I suggest, "Let's order in."

Chapter 34

Lana

Graduation. That was when I found out. After the ceremony, we went out to celebrate. I remembered getting too drunk and waking up on the floor, hearing a bed creak beside me. Trying to keep still and figure out where I was, I realized I was in my room. Then I heard the moaning. I heard the words *I love you*. I lay there listening to Alicia and Maksim fucking on my bed, hoping it was just a dream, but I never woke up.

I watched Alicia and Maksim living out the life I was supposed to have. Maksim was my high school sweetheart, and he promised me forever. We met Alicia in college, but she and I were never close. She and Maksim had the same major, so their schedule always matched up. He promised me they were just friends and convinced me we were all good friends, but I never hung out with her alone. Now here they are together as a family. If I ever have to explain heartbreak, it will feel like losing someone you love, but that someone is yourself, and you know you'll never get that part of you back.

When I finally snap out of it, I see them being escorted away.

"Let's go," Adrian says softly, and I follow his lead.

Stepping onto a golf cart, we are driven away from the building and toward another area on the property. The sign we pass says *The Andromeda Residence*. This section is perfectly spaced out homes to have a more personalized experience.

It is a serene oasis. We pull up to one of the homes and are given a key card. Stepping into a tastefully decorated home, featuring elegant furnishings and subtle hues that create a calming ambiance. Large windows allow natural light to flood the open living space, enhancing the feeling of spaciousness. The modern kitchen is equipped for culinary adventures, and a dining area overlooks the sea, perfect for enjoying meals with a view.

"I'll take our bags to the master bedroom," Adrian says to me.

I shoot him a smile while I continue to walk through the home. As I step onto the expansive sea-view sun terrace, a stunning view of the sparkling Mediterranean Sea greets us. The private infinity pool shimmers under the setting sun, seamlessly blending with the horizon. This is a sanctuary away from the world, where every moment feels like a luxurious escape in paradise.

I make my way back inside and into our bedroom to find Adrian on the balcony looking out at another stunning view. Standing beside him, I grip the railing.

"Do you like sushi?" Adrian asks. "I'll have dinner sent over."

"That sounds good," I reply.

"Do you want to talk about it?"

"About dinner?"

"About Tweedledee and Tweedledum."

My cheeks flush. "I'd rather not. It was over a decade ago. And you pretty much had it right."

Turning to face me, Adrian leans on the railing with his hips. Crossing his arms, his biceps look bigger than usual. "Just say the word, Lana."

Pushing off the rail, I place my hands on my hips. "You can't just go live life killing anyone that upsets you."

"Well, someone should have told me that sooner." This devilish, handsome smile crosses his unapologetic face.

I attempt to hold back a laugh but fail. "He's not worth it."

"But you are." He closes the gap between us, cupping my face with his massive hands.

"Getting soft on me?"

"I'm trying, Lana. Give me some grace." His thumb caresses my cheek. "I didn't know you had it so rough."

"Not as rough as you have."

"For men, it builds character. Women are to be spoiled."

I smile. "Like I said, you've shown me more kindness than anyone has. You don't have to try so hard."

His mouth gently comes down onto mine. The gentleness in his kiss is the complete opposite of what I am used to. His plump lips are like cushions, and I find myself leaning into him. Those strong arms of his wrap around my body, giving me a sense of safety. The doorbell puts this intimate moment on pause. When he pulls away, I feel my body wanting to chase him.

"Go down by the pool," Adrian says as he goes to answer the door.

As I walk back down to the pool, confusion sets in once

again. Kind, gentle, and soft are not adjectives I'd ever use to describe Adrian, yet now he is showing me a completely different side. Taking a seat on one of the comfortable loungers under the shaded cabana, I wait while soft, rhythmic waves from the sea provide a soothing soundtrack.

Adrian comes into view with a waiter walking behind him. On the waiter's shoulder is a large heart-shaped dish that he places on a table under the cabana. On it is a selection of uramaki, hosomaki, nigiri, and sashimi placed strategically in the center of the platter. The outline of the dish is decorated with mango, carob, grapes, prickly pears, papaya, guava, carambola, pitahaya, and jackfruit paired with petit fours.

The waiter places a large bottle of Billecart Salmon Brut Rosé champagne on the table that he holds in his hand before securing the platter from his shoulder onto the table. Once the platter is secure, he opens the bottle. Once everything is perfectly set, he bows to us. Adrian hands him a tip and waves him away.

We sit, and Adrian makes a toast.

"To the fools who lost us."

I clink my cup to his and we both watch each other as we sip our drinks.

"You have a story?" I ask.

"I have many stories."

"I want to hear your heartbreak story."

Adrian laughs. "I'm usually the one breaking hearts."

I shake my head. "There's always one that changes you. Shapes your understanding of love."

He remains poised, but I know there is one in there. I'm going to pry it out of him, but to my surprise, he gives in voluntarily.

"We were set to marry. I get tossed into prison, and she

marries someone else on the same date that ours was set. Can't blame her—five years is a long time."

I take a piece of mango off the platter. "You seem at peace with it."

"It takes more energy to hate someone. I'd rather use it toward important things."

Biting into the mango, its sweet juices coat my mouth. "It must have been rough."

"At first, then I got over it."

"I mean prison. It must have been rough." I swallow the mango in anticipation. "It's unheard of to be sent to the Black Dolphin and make it out alive."

"Maybe that's why I lack fear. There's nowhere and no one worse that can compare to a place or people like that."

Adrian eats the fish in whole bites, and I find it oddly satisfying watching him eat. The muscles in his arms and neck flex.

"Now you're the one staring," Adrian acknowledges.

I clear my throat and grab a sashimi to take a bite.

"There is something I want you to answer honestly."

The feel of the sashimi down my throat almost chokes me. "What would that be?"

"Did you mean what you said last night?"

Instantly, I feel my stomach drop. I thought him ignoring it was bothersome, but now that he's acknowledging it, I want to run.

"What did I say?"

He smiles. "So you want to play stupid now."

"No," I reply, trying to laugh it off. "It was just in the heat of the moment."

He nods his head. "Okay." There's a sense of disappointment in his voice.

"Does it really matter?"

"No. We are married, Lana—till death do us part. You don't have to love me."

Adrian gets up and heads toward the pool, taking the champagne bottle with him. He doesn't ask for me to follow, but it feels as though I should. It is still light out, but soon enough, the sky will begin to darken. Removing my sandals, I hike up my dress and dip my feet in. Taking a deep breath, inhaling the soothing scents, I allow the world around me to fade. The tension of the last few days has taken a toll on me more than I expected. I've been barely married a week, and so much has taken place.

Adrian removes his shoes and places his feet in the pool beside mine, handing me the bottle of champagne. I take it, have a chug, then hand it back to him.

"Growing up, my father would make Gil and I fight each other until one of us got knocked out," Adrian confesses out of nowhere, then hands the bottle back to me.

"Growing up, if my mother thought I was being diffi-cult, she wouldn't let me eat." Putting the bottle to my lips and taking a big chug.

Adrian takes the bottle from me when I am done. "I had to cancel my eighteenth birthday pool party because my father needed to hide bodies after a last minute slaughter."

"I was forced to drop out of medical school to marry Beau because my father lost a bet."

Adrian hands me the bottle as a signal that I have topped that one. I don't know what sparked this conversa-tion, but it seems as though Adrian is trying anyway he knows how to connect. We both need to. I can't help but wonder if he is always this way or if prison changed him.

"A doctor? You should go back to school."

Laughing at the idea, I shake my head. "It was just to be

away from the house. Intense schooling and being an attending was the only excuse I had for that bit of freedom."

Taking the bottle from me, he goes on, "Sometimes I wish I weren't a Sokolov."

It may have been the most honest thing that has come out of his mouth, and it feels like his confession has freed him from something that is holding him back.

"Most times, I wish I weren't a Petrova."

"Well, now you're a Sokolov, so cheers to that."

Something shifts. We look at one another with an understanding, an appreciation for surviving our struggles, and we spend most of the night learning more about what makes us who we are. When the sky is at its darkest point, I find myself placing my head on his shoulder.

Chapter 35

Adrian

The sound of waves crashing onto shore in the distance is soothing, but my mind drifts far away, back to a time that seemed both distant and vivid. I can almost hear the gentle clatter of pots and pans, the sound of my grandmother's apron rustling as she moved about the room.

It was a small kitchen, the walls painted a cheerful yellow, the air tinged with the comforting aroma of her famous apple pie. My grandmother, Clara, had always been the heart of my world, nurturing me in ways I didn't fully understand until much later. She was more of a mother to me than my own.

I was perched on a stool at the kitchen counter, painfully shy and unsure of how to connect with my peers. I fiddled with the edge of my shirt, feeling small. Just as I was about to voice my concerns, my grandmother turned to me with her warm smile, which felt like a blanket wrapping around me.

"Adrian, sweetheart, come here." She beckoned me with a tender voice, her bright gray eyes sparkling with wisdom. I hopped off the stool and shuffled over to her side, drawn by her magnetism, her ability to make me feel seen.

"Do you remember the story I told you about the sunshine and the rain?" she asked, kneeling down to meet my gaze.

I nodded, the memory rushing back of her explaining how both elements were essential for life to flourish, just as trust was critical for relationships.

"People are like plants, my love," my grandmother continued with her soothing voice. "They can bloom beautifully, but they need kindness, patience, and warmth to open up. Do you understand?"

I furrowed my brow slightly, not entirely grasping what she meant. She gestured for me to sit on the kitchen floor, and I complied, eager to be near her.

"Let me show you," she said, pulling out a worn-out journal filled with their favorite recipes and moments. "This journal is special, just like our conversations. You see these pages? Each one tells a story, much like the people you meet every day."

She opened the journal to a page where a recipe for chocolate chip cookies lay, a space filled with notes in her delicate handwriting. "When you share something personal, like a recipe or a memory, it encourages others to share in return. It builds trust, Adrian."

With careful precision, she pointed at the handwritten notes. "Watch, I'll show you. If I say, 'I once baked these cookies for a neighbor who felt lonely,' it invites curiosity, doesn't it?"

I nodded, intrigued by her words. She had a way of making everything feel like magic.

"And just like that, when you talk to someone—whether it's a friend or someone new—share a little about yourself first. Open the door to your heart, and they'll find it easier to open theirs, too."

She placed a gentle hand on my shoulder. "Remember, trust is a two-way street. Be genuine, and people will want to connect. You have a good heart, Adrian. Never forget that."

"Okay, babushka." I sighed. A swell of affection mixed with understanding filled me with the love and intention behind her words.

"I know it's tough being your father's son. The pressure and the expectation to be like him or better." She placed a kiss on my forehead.

As I hugged her, a cough erupted from within her, causing her to cover her mouth. Rushing to grab her a napkin, she wiped away blood from her hands.

"You're bleeding, yaya!"

"I coughed too hard," she smiled, though she seemed to wince in pain. "Why don't you go play with your brother and sister?"

Although I was hesitant, I could tell she really wanted to be alone. Sprinting for the door, I stopped at the sound of her body hitting the floor.

* * *

I quickly wipe a tear that threatens to slip free. My grandmother's wisdom has shaped me, helping me navigate through the complexities of human emotion and relationships when I was a young boy. Despite the passing years, her lessons remain etched in my heart.

Lana lays her head on my shoulder, and I feel her body relax next to mine. It's been so long since I've had a decent conversation with a woman. She opened up to me, which was my goal, but the result of it wasn't what I expected. Taking my grandmother's advice, I was taken aback by the outcome. Lana shared more than expected, and our conversation lingered in the back of my mind, weaving its way through my reflections like a soft melody. I thought, having grown up in the bratva, we would share similar stories, yet she made it clear how awful her family treated her. Unlike my sister Bianca, who was given everything she wanted and more, Lana was treated like an inconvenience. Our talk opened my eyes to layers of her being that I had yet to explore.

I take her in my arms and carry her to bed. Watching her sleep somehow relaxes me. It's always easy to take someone's strength for granted, and I underestimated the weight Lana carries with her. She unveiled her vulnerabilities; the way she spoke about her childhood and the moments that shaped her created a new level of respect I have for her.

"I felt invisible most times," Lana admits, *"Like being daughter of Andre Petrov meant I had to be strong all the time, but inside I was just a little girl wanting to be seen and cry when my feelings were hurt."*

I admire her honesty. Now, when she smiles, I see how it hides a spectrum of emotions, how the gentle caress of her laughter sometimes masks deeper insecurities. I realize that part of getting her to fall in love with me needs to include understanding the shadows she has walked in and making sure she never feels outcasted again.

Walking out of the bedroom, I call the front desk.

"Mr. Sokolov, how may I help you?"

"That couple that was tossed out earlier today. I want their name and address."

Chapter 36

Lana

Opening my eyes, I find myself in bed. A pounding in my head keeps me from getting up. On the nightstand beside me, there is a cup of water and Tylenol. Forcing myself to sit up, I take both, hoping for a quick recovery. That's when I see it. Grabbing a photograph off the nightstand, I see it's old. It's a picture of me, Alicia, and Maksim, except Maksim's face is burned off. Quickly getting to my feet, I run out of the room. Adrian isn't in the house. When I hear splashing outside, I run onto the terrace.

Adrian is swimming laps, and I stand at the edge of the pool, waiting for him to pop his head up. When he does, he stands on his feet, pushing his wet hair back, his muscles flexing with every movement.

"Good morning, wife."

"What did you do!?"

"I ordered breakfast and came for a swim. I wasn't going to wake you up."

Holding up the photo to his face, I question again, "I'm talking about this."

Adrian takes the photo and starts getting out of the pool. As he does, he examines the photo as though seeing it for the first time. "What about it?"

"Adrian."

He lifts my chin with his finger. "I may not be good with words, but you can rely on my actions."

"He has children."

"I kept her alive."

I should be nauseated by this, but I find it charming, and now I'm convinced I may be just as crazy as he is.

"What were you trying to say with your actions with this?"

"That I will eliminate whoever has hurt you, is going to hurt, or will hurt you. As your husband, I promise you that."

His hands glide down my arms, his touch firm yet tender, as if he is mapping my body, claiming it as his own.

"Beautiful," he murmurs, his fingers tracing the curve of my shoulder, down my arm, and back up to my waist as he circles behind me.

His touch is deliberate, possessive, as if he is etching me into his memory. I shiver, my body responding to his every movement, nipples tightening into hard peaks. Stepping closer, his body presses against mine, his hardness a promise against my lower back. I feel his lips on my shoulder, his teeth grazing my skin, sending sparks of pleasure through me. His hands move down, cupping my breasts, thumbing my nipples until I gasp, my head falling back to give him better access. He kisses his way down my neck, his breath hot against my skin, his hands relentless in their exploration.

"Can I do that for you, Lana?" he asks with his voice rough as his lips brush my earlobe. "Protect you at all costs?"

My body comes to life. "Okay," I whisper with a trembling voice. "But no more killing."

He chuckles, a low, dark sound that sends a shiver of thrill down my spine. "I can't promise you that."

I want to protest, but the desire is too strong to hold back. "You're stubborn. You can't—"

He cuts me off with a kiss, his lips demanding, his tongue invading my mouth, tasting me, owning me. Pulling down the straps of my sundress that I'm still wearing from yesterday, I help remove it by pulling it down my body until it pools around my feet as Adrian sucks on my neck, holding onto my breasts for dear life. His hands move lower, sliding down my stomach, his fingers teasing the sensitive skin of my inner thighs. I whimper, my legs trembling as he spreads them apart, his touch deliberate as he pushes my lace panties to the side and begins brushing against my slit.

"So wet for me," he growls, his breath hot against my neck. "I think you like the monster in me."

His fingers slide inside me, slow and deep, his thumb pressing against my clit, sending waves of pleasure crashing through me, panting as my body arches into his touch while my hips move of their own accord. He works me with precision, his fingers relentless, his thumb circling, pressing, teasing until I'm a mess of moans and gasps, my body trembling on the edge.

"Go on now, admit it."

"Adrian," my voice is desperate.

"Lana," he urges.

His fingers continue their relentless rhythm, pushing me closer, holding me on the edge. My body is a coil wound tight, every nerve ending screaming for release, but he is denying me, his control absolute.

"Say it," he demands, his voice harsh, his breath hot

against my ear. "Tell me how much you enjoy the demons in me."

My eyes widen as my body trembles with need. I want to protest, but the words catch in my throat, my breath coming in short, desperate gasps as his thick fingers work their magic.

"I love it," I moan.

He laughs, a dark, satisfied sound. "That's my good girl."

Just like that, I am unraveled. He works me with precision, his fingers relentless, diving in and out of me, his thumb continues circling, pressing, and teasing, as more moans and gasps until my body melts into his as my orgasm erupts out of me. Adrian holds me up, his erection solid against my lower back. Once my legs stop trembling and I am able to stand straight, he makes his way in front of me.

His wet hair still dripping water down his perfectly framed face and sculpted body sends a new flood of desire through me. I watch as he looks at his hand, covered in my cum, and licks it off his skin. Mumbling something to himself, his eyes snap up to mine, and his lips flicker with a subtle twitch. Taking my hand, he leads me to a lounger where he lies on his back with his hands behind his head. I gaze at Adrian, completely captivated by the striking art that seems to echo the beauty of his form. The scars and tattoos that adorn his muscular body tell stories of battles fought and won, each mark adding to his rugged charm. His muscular legs are weapons of their own. His sculpted torso, bulging biceps, and veiny arms transition seamlessly into a strong neck, exuding both strength and masculinity. Lying there, Adrian appears bold and fearless, like a trophy, showing off his years as not only a bratva king but the essence of a true warrior. Perhaps allowing myself to fall for him won't be so daunting. I'm willing to take my time getting there if he's willing to keep me safe like he promises.

Adrian lies there and patiently waits as I stand at the end of the lounger. With his feet on the ground and his legs wide open, his erection stands tall through his swim trunks, inviting me to play. I slowly crawl toward his cock, placing one knee on the lounger and both hands gripping the edge of the lounger on each side of his thighs. I watch his chest rise and fall with steady breaths. His body is relaxed, but I know better than to mistake his calm for weakness. I already feel the force of his power, the way he can unravel me with just a touch. Now, it's my turn to dismantle him, to peel back his layers and expose the raw, vulnerable core beneath.

His dark lashes make his gray eyes pop as he watches me with a mixture of amusement and anticipation. His hair, damp from the pool, clings to his forehead, and a faint sheen of sweat glistens on his skin. Again, my eyes trail down his body—the lean muscles of his chest, the defined lines of his abs, the thick, long, veiny cock of his aching to be released. His lips curve into a small, knowing smile.

I lean forward, my hands resting lightly on his thighs. His skin is warm under my palms, and I feel the faint tremor of his muscles as he shifts beneath my touch. Slowly, deliberately, I trail my fingers upward, tracing the contours of his body until I reach the waistband of his swim trunks.

"Relax," I softly speak, my breath ghosting over his skin. "This is my show now."

Adrian's hand grips the top edge of the lounger, his knuckles whitening as he fights the urge to move. I hook my fingers into the elastic of his trunks and pull them down, baring him to my gaze. His cock bursts out, finally free from his garment, glistening with pre-cum.

I take a moment to admire him, my eyes lingering on

the way his skin flushes with arousal. Then, with a slow, deliberate motion, I lean forward, my lips brushing the sensitive skin of his inner thigh. Adrian's breath hitches, and I feel a surge of satisfaction at the way his body is reacting to me.

"Lana..." he warns, his voice rough, but I ignore him, pressing a soft kiss to the base of his cock before looking up at him through my lashes.

"Mmhmm," I hum with fingers wrapping gently around his shaft, dragging my tongue up to the head.

"Show me—"

This time, I make sure to cut him off as I take him in my mouth, slowly and deliberately, savoring the taste and texture of him. My tongue traces every ridge and curve, mapping his cock with a familiarity that makes him shudder. I tighten my grip, keeping my lips firm, and begin to move with a rhythm that is both relentless and teasing. My free hand strokes his thigh, anchoring him as I deepen the pressure, pulling him further into her mouth.

Adrian's breath quickens, his chest heaving as he fights to maintain control. Glancing up at him, I watch him through half-lidded eyes, relishing the way his body tenses, the way now both his hands grip the top edge of the lounger like it's the only thing keeping him grounded. His moans are muffled by his own mouth, and I smile with a hum against his skin, allowing the vibrations to send shivers through him.

"Fuck, Lana..." he groans, his voice thick with need.

I hum deeper in response, my tongue swirling around the tip of his cock before I let it pop out of my mouth, teasing him with slow, deliberate licks. His hips twitch, and I press both hands down onto his thigh, holding him still and taking him all the way in. Drool mixed with pre-cum pours out of my mouth as I lower my head until my nose touches his pelvis.

This sends a jolt through him, and I feel his body tremble beneath my touch as I try not to gag. Slowly lifting my head up, then taking him back fully into my mouth and down my throat, my rhythm is steady and relentless, driving him closer to the edge with every stroke. Taking one hand, I cup his balls, my thumb brushing the sensitive area.

Adrian's moans grow louder, his body arching off the lounger as he struggles to hold back. His reaction is what is keeping me going, my lips and tongue working in perfect harmony to push him further. His hands tangle in my hair, tugging gently as he calls me his goddess.

"Moya boginya." His voice raw and desperate.

My throat tightens around him as I continue taking him in as far as I can and massaging his balls. His hips buck as I proudly drive him closer to the edge. Adrian's body tenses, his muscles locking as he cries out, his release spilling into her mouth. Taking it all in, my lips move in time with his tremors, milking every last drop from him. His hands loosen around my hair, his body going limp as he surrenders to the aftermath of his orgasm.

Sitting up on my knee, wiping the drool and cum around my mouth with the back of my hand, I watch Adrian lie shattered, his chest heaving as he stares up at the sky, his eyes dilated with pleasure. I can't hold back a satisfied smile on my lips as I look down at him.

"That's what you'll call me from now on," I say with a voice laced in triumph.

He manages a weak laugh, his hand reaching out to brush my hair from my face. "You keep doing that, and I will call you whatever you want," he admits with a hoarse voice.

The doorbell rings and Adrian gets up, wraps a towel around his godly body, and lets the waiter in while I jump in the pool to cool off. Once the waiter sees me, he wastes no time in delivering breakfast and sees himself out. This time, the heart shaped platter full of berries, Bircher muesli, some chi pudding with coconut, and pearl barley drizzled with honey is placed in the pool, becoming a floating dish. In the ice bucket is Philipponnat Royale Reserve champagne that Adrian pops open, removes his towel, and gets into the pool with me.

"We aren't leaving this pool until my cock falls off."

Chapter 37

Adrian

I am balls deep in Lana, loving hearing her screaming that I'm her god. The splashing of the water around us, causing the platter to spill food into the pool, the sun beating on our skin, or how the water has wrinkled our skin like raisins can't stop us from ravishing one another. Lana's nails claw into my back as we both climax for the umpteenth time today. Pinning her against the wall of the pool, I bury my head into her neck as our hearts both settle down.

"I need a break," Lana says, her voice slightly breathless, lips a shade of blue from the cool water of the pool.

"Afternoon snack?" I suggest, one eyebrow raised in playful inquiry.

"Something light. Don't want to spoil dinner." She smiles, a playful glint in her eye, her intent clear as she glances back at me.

I follow behind her as we climb out of the pool, my gaze drawn to the way the sunlight glistens off her skin, beads of water cascading down her curves—fueling my craving for more, even though I too desperately need a pause. Just as I reach for a towel, the shrill ring of my phone pierces the air.

I roll my eyes when I see it's my brother.

"What do you want?" My tone carries irritation, the annoyance evident as I try to shake off the lingering distraction.

"You know your dick can get sunburned, right?" he says, amusement lacing his words.

"What?" I glance around, alert, scanning the area to ensure Gil isn't lurking nearby.

"Your dick. Sunburnt. Not fun. And I'm speaking from experience." His laughter resonates through the phone.

"Where the fuck are you?" My voice rises instinctively, a mix of concern and exasperation, causing Lana to look up at me, her brow furrowing.

"Relax, Adrian. I didn't crash your little freak-off," Gil chuckles.

Taking my towel, I toss it over to Lana, my frustration surfacing in an almost playful gesture. "What the fuck, Gil?" Looking at the exterior of the house, I can only guess one thing. My voice drops to a conspiratorial whisper, "Did you put cameras here?"

"Well, after buying that specific house, I wanted to ensure no one else would use it," he replies nonchalantly.

"How long have you been watching?" I wrap a towel around my waist, feeling the tension in my shoulders tighten.

"Somewhere in between the *bozhe moy* and the *ne prekrashchay trakhat' menya*," he responds, his tone mockingly proud.

"What is wrong with you?" I feel my blood pressure rise.

"I only jerked off once." His smirk seems to filter through the phone.

"Gil." I raise my middle finger, hoping the unseen camera catches my gesture.

He laughs. "Okay, okay, twice. For a man who's been in prison for a while, you sure know how to make a woman scream."

"It has sound, too?" My irritation boils over.

"No, but now I'm thinking I should have gotten audio for the cameras. It would have really added to the show."

"I'm going to kill you," I grind out, my irritation palpable.

"It's only on the outside. The inside is clear," he adds with a pause, "Possibly."

"Gil."

"You have me locked up in my house. I'm bored out of my mind."

"You, too, have a wife," I remind him, the frustration mingling with the absurdity of the situation.

"She's in a pissy mood. I did give you guys our weekend there, and she's taking it out on me."

"Turn off the cameras."

"Love you too, brother." He hangs up, leaving me seething with annoyance. As I strut back toward Lana, lounging under the cabana, I swipe my phone, calling for a late lunch.

"Mr. Sokolov, how may we assist you?" the voice from the intercom chirps.

"Bring us an Alaskan king crab with lemon and crème fraîche. Throw in some macaroons and salted butter caramel scones," I order, ensuring my voice remains composed.

"May I recommend R de Ruinart? This champagne will pair very well with the crab."

"Perfect," I reply, allowing a small smile to surface.

I settle onto the sunbed beside Lana, both of us lying back, gazing through the sheer curtain draping over the cabana.

"Is everything okay?" she asks, her voice laced with concern and curiosity.

"Just Gil being...Gil." I gesture dismissively, though a hint of a smile tugs at my lips.

She lets out a light laugh, the sound echoing sweetly. "He's an interesting one."

"I'm sure he'll make a pass at you at some point," I say, half-joking, half-serious.

She turns her head to meet my gaze, surprise flickering in her eyes. "What? I'm your wife; he's your brother!"

"He's Gil. I give you full permission to kill him if he does," I say, teasing yet earnest.

"I wouldn't think he'd be the one to make a move," she muses, looking back at the ceiling with a thoughtful expression. "Raya has been oddly touchy."

"Not surprising. Raya and Gil are made for each other," I reply, shaking my head.

"Has she made a move on you?" Her voice lowers, a hint of trepidation slipping through.

"She makes a pass at everyone—just put her in her place," I advise, reassuringly.

"Do I need to worry?"

"About Raya?" I shake my head vigorously. "She's selfish but not stupid. I've made it clear that if she comes near me, I will decapitate her."

Lana fiddles with her chain necklace, the sun casting intricate shadows on her skin, leaving a faint tan line. I sit up on my elbow, a sudden impulse driving me as I reach out, breaking the necklace chain off her neck.

"You don't need this anymore," I declare, tossing the chain aside.

We lie there in comfortable silence until our food arrives. "Let's eat on the balcony," I suggest, pointing to our room above.

After having the waiter set up the table on the balcony, we take our seats, picking up our champagne glasses.

"To you, Lana," I raise my glass high, feeling the weight of the moment.

"To you, Adrian," she responds, a soft smile illuminating her features.

We clink our glasses, savoring the taste of celebration, and I catch a swirl of seduction reflecting in her eyes.

"Did you bring your toy?" I ask, a teasing note in my voice.

"I'll go get it," she replies, excitement dancing in her eyes.

I gulp down my drink, typing a few text messages as I wait. When she returns, something mysterious is in her hands.

"Did you put this in my bag?" she asks, flipping it around to reveal a Queen of Spades.

Chapter 38

Lana

In twenty-four hours, I've seen Adrian in ways I couldn't have anticipated, but the image that will etch itself into my memory is that moment when I show him the Queen of Spades.

"Where did you find that?" he demands, his voice a low growl as he rises abruptly from his chair, tension radiating off him like heat waves.

"It was in my bag," I reply, my heart racing, anxiety pooling in my stomach.

His eyes darken, his jaw tightening. "Pack your bag. We are leaving. Now." The urgency in his voice sends an icy shiver down my spine.

Dashing into our room, he maintains a calm exterior while frantically making a call. I only catch snippets— "family meeting, leaving tonight," his tone sharp and unyielding, "don't say a word." Within thirty minutes, we're packed and heading to the airport. A Queen of Spades isn't just a playing card; it's a symbol of death, and a chilling realization washes over me: who is threatening me? Have others received one too?

"Are you going to tell me what's going on?" I push, my voice tinged with desperation.

"You don't know what a Queen of Spades means?" His eyes flash with a mix of anger and fear.

"Well, yes, but...who would try to threaten me?" I counter, my voice trembling slightly, uncertainty clenching my throat.

"Who wants you dead?" he shoots back, the intensity between us electric yet fraught with tension.

We spiral into a barrage of questions, yet the answers remain elusive.

"What now?" My heart races, the weight of the unknown pressing down on us.

"Let me handle it," Adrian states with palpable authority. "I told you I will protect you—so let me do that. Okay?"

"Okay," I reply, my voice small, feeling cornered with no clear alternatives.

Once we arrive in Moscow, Adrian's Ferrari awaits us, a sleek reminder of the life we had momentarily stepped away from. When we enter the house, his family waits anxiously, relief flooding their features as they see us walk in hand in hand, unharmed—albeit tense.

"Adrian," his father stands abruptly, panic lacing his words. "We should leave the city."

"And go where?" Bianca demands, her demeanor equally frantic.

"You all may leave if you want, but I am staying here. This is my city," Adrian asserts, his voice resolute but laced with defiance.

"Adrian, don't be stubborn," my mother begs, desperation seeping into her tone as she steps closer, her hands raised in a placating gesture.

"You should have stayed in Cyprus," Gil chimes in, eyes narrowed with reproach.

"So you can spy on me?" Adrian snaps back, irritation bloating beneath his calm facade.

"Can't you set up a trap or something?" Raya adds, her voice laced with impatience.

"Easier said than done," Adrian replies, exasperation creeping into his voice.

He stands beside me, his grip on my hand possessive, thumb stroking my skin in a futile attempt to soothe both of our nerves as the discussion around us escalates into chaos.

"Instead of hiding, we should be out in public as much as possible," I interject, adrenaline pumping through me—I have no real plan, but instinct tells me hiding will never draw out whoever threatened us.

"This all started with you," his father seethes, eyes glinting with blame.

"It has nothing to do with her," Adrian fires back, his voice unwavering, eyes blazing as he defends me.

"How do you know?" His mother interjects sharply, her gaze flickering between us.

"Lana wouldn't have gotten a threat," Adrian counters fiercely, standing tall.

"Unless she's trying not to look guilty," Bianca's voice drips with anger, her frustration palpable.

The tension in the room builds, allowing fear to seep in as everyone speaks over each other, escalating nerves churning like a brewing storm.

"Enough!" Adrian roars, rising to his feet. He releases my hand, slamming his palms down on the table, his posture emanating authority. The room falls silent, tension hanging thick in the air. "This is not the time to bicker. We can't risk weakness between us."

"You're absolutely right, Adrian." A proud smile breaks on his father's face, as if proud of his son's fierce spirit.

Just as we expect him to outline a plan, the tranquility shatters like fragile glass. The heavy wooden doors of the dining hall swing open with violent force, crashing against the stone walls. In an instant, a group of men bursts in—armed, relentless, their eyes cold with fury.

The previously squabbling family now shares a collective panic, terror flooding our veins. Adrian, Gil, and their father spring into action without hesitation—drawing their weapons as if on instinct. I watch as Adrian reaches beneath the table, retrieving a .50 BMG pistol with an unsettling ease, his eyes sharp and alert while pointing it toward the encroaching threat.

The women, filled with dread, scramble for cover, crawling under the table, unable to escape this escalating nightmare.

Ivan and Sergei rush in, bringing additional reinforcements as chaos erupts—blood splatters across the room, fists fly, and bodies crash to the ground. Bianca's terrified screeches blend with the cacophony of violence, while her mother clings to her, desperate to shield her from the reality of our situation. Raya and I cling to each other, trembling in fear, wishing for a window to escape this perilous trap.

A merciless stillness envelops the room like a slowly tightening noose, lingering only for a moment before the suffocating silence is interrupted by Bianca's sobs echoing in our ears.

"Come out, come out wherever you are," a chilling voice resonates, reverberating against the walls as footsteps creep closer to the table.

"We are going to die," Ivanka whispers beside me, trembling, "And it's your fault."

Fear seizes me as we watch a pair of legs halt in front of us. A man kneels down, revealing a maniacal grin that sends shivers down my spine.

"Why don't you ladies come out to play?" he taunts, voice dripping with malice.

When we remain stubbornly hidden, his men start yanking us out from our shelters, forcing us to stand in a grim line. Across from us stand Adrian, Gil, Ivan, Sergei, and a couple of men, guns drawn and faces taut with disbelief and fury.

Ivanka's horrified scream pierces the air as she spots her husband lying lifelessly on the floor. Instinctively, both she and Bianca lunge forward, but guns are raised threateningly, and they halt, fear choking their movements.

A man, as tall as I am, towers in front of me. "Lana Petrova. Finally, nice to meet you," he sneers.

I struggle to maintain composure, though the tremor in my hands betrays my nerves. The man slowly traces his finger from my temple down my jawline, lingering at my chin as he reveals the Queen of Spades, a twisted smile carving his features.

"Three people were given this," he announces nonchalantly, "one of them is dead."

"Has your mother taught you no manners?" I retort, trying to mask my fear with sarcasm. "You barge into our home without a gift and make all this mess."

With a sadistic smile revealing a mouth filled with gold teeth, the man raises the back of his hand, striking my face with a brutal speed that stings deep.

"Don't touch her!" Adrian's voice booms as he struggles

against the five men gripping him back, his fury tangible, even with a gun aimed at his head.

Ignoring Adrian's demands, the man extends his hand toward me. Reluctantly, I take it, dread pooling in the pit of my stomach as he leads me to the center of the room. A harsh shove from one of his men leaves Gil standing beside me, arms crossed, his expression tense yet defiant. I can feel my body growing weaker, shaking as fear threatens to overcome me.

The man gestures to his crew, and one of them thrusts a gun into my hand while another places one in Gil's grip. "Let's play a game," he announces gleefully, circling us like a predator stalking its prey. "Who loves Russian roulette?"

A chill runs through me, my body numb as I process the reality of our situation. Gil and I are forced to stand back to back.

"Can't off someone all by yourself?" Gil jests, yet the quaver in his voice betrays his fear.

The man grows visibly irritated, yet continues, "There's one bullet in there. The person who shoots the other gets to live."

"What's the caveat?" Gil probes, aware of the man's hidden agenda.

"You can swap someone in your place, giving your life for another's. But don't get stupid; one wrong move, and everyone in this room will die."

Panic begins to swell inside me like a suffocating cloud, and I struggle to steady my breath. Time seems to slow, the chaos of the room morphing into a distant hum as dread envelops me.

"Lana, darling," the man croons, his voice sickly sweet. "Pay attention—your life is on the line." He snaps his fingers in front of my face, jolting me back to the harrowing reality. "Who do you wish to take your place?"

My gaze turns blank; I'm too stunned to respond.

"Lana! Focus!" he shouts, the urgency in his tone spiking my anxiety. "Pick someone in this room."

I shake my head, panic squeezing at my throat as I realize the gravity of the decision before me. I don't want to bear that weight, knowing there are lives at stake—Adrian and I have finally begun to connect. I can't choose his family member to die.

"If you don't pick, I will pick for you," he threatens, his gaze flickering over my shoulder, and I feel the dread of destination looming as I suspect he's referring to Adrian.

"Ivanka," I blurt out, name escaping like a whisper of betrayal.

"Going after mommy dearest," he laughs cruelly before turning to Gil. "Your turn, kid."

With my back turned to Gil, I can't see his expression, but I sense him stall, not from uncertainty in picking someone but from the emotional weight of the choice ahead. The eyes of Ivanka, who clutches at her heart, Bianca, who is desperately wiping her tears, and Raya, who looks as if her spirit has been crushed, haunt me.

"Adrian," Gil finally states with a chilling sense of certainty.

Gasps fill the room; a son, a brother, a friend will be lost today—all while I mentally prepare my own death certificate. If Adrian dies, I'm back to square one, circling the drain without a way out.

"Let's begin," the man says with guttural joy, initiating the countdown. "Five steps and shoot."

As he counts, I take wide steps, each one akin to a relentless hammer pounding on my chest.

"One. Two. Three. Four. Five."

Turning, I spin the gun, not aiming at Gil, but rather at the man before us. If Gil isn't going to end my life, surely this man will pursue me. With a final surge of resolve, I shut my eyes, pulling the trigger, bracing for Gil's bullet to find me instead.

Then, all I hear is chaos erupting—a cacophony of screams. As I open my eyes, I see the man being tackled by Ivan, while Adrian is on top of Gil, punching his face into a bloody pulp.

"Lana," Sergei calls, urgency flooding his voice. "Let's go."

Chapter 39

Adrian

Pacing around the room, I drink from a bottle of vodka with one hand, a different taste than the champagne I was having a few hours ago, while holding an ice packet to my face with my other hand.

A light knock on the frame of the entrance causes me to look up.

"Shouldn't you be tending to your husband?"

Raya's expression is cold. "My husband, your brother, is fine. Just needs to rest up."

"He has his own home to do that in."

"Adrian, you know Gil loves you. You need to hear him out—understand his way of thinking."

"Raya, I think his actions were very clear. I won't have Lana around that."

"Don't tell me you're in love with that fragile thing." Raya's expression remains stone-cold, yet I can sense the turmoil boiling beneath her placid facade. It gnaws at her, a searing wound that refuses to heal, when she sees Lana and me together.

"What's that matter to you?" Pulling out a cigar, I sit on my big leather cushioned chair.

Gliding across the room, the black satin fabric of her dress moves along her skin with each stride. The sight used to melt me, but now I see her as a desperate fool.

"You're punishing me," she says, her voice laced with accusation, an unspoken plea lurking in her eyes.

I flick the lighter, the flame momentarily illuminating my face. I place the cigar between my lips, inhaling deeply before exhaling a cloud of smoke, each puff a silent challenge.

"What reason do I have to punish you?" I counter, my voice steady as I savor the burn of the tobacco.

"I had no choice, Adrian." Her voice remains delicate as she approaches me. "You know that."

"No one held a gun to your head."

We lock eyes, mine sending waves of betrayal while hers held pity. A moment passes, heavy and suffocating, as we hold our gaze. Her eyes shimmer with barely concealed pity, as if she is the martyr in this twisted tale.

"You went to prison, Adrian. I had no one to take care of me."

"All you had to do was wait for me," I shoot back, my voice hardening.

The smoke from the cigar swirls in the air around us.

"Gil said you were going to die in there. Everyone expected you to die."

"You had no faith in me." I let out a huff of air through my nose, the bitterness of her betrayal lingering on my tongue.

Then, in a moment that shatters the tension, she sinks to

her knees, placing her hands on my thighs for support, searching for the warmth that has long since faded. "I was going to be thrown out into the streets. I married Gil for survival, but my heart is yours." Her voice falters as she looks up at me, filled with longing and desperation. "It always will be. You're my one and only."

Placing the cigar in my mouth, I smirk. "Let me guess... Gil convinced you."

"No," she shakes her head. "Your father. He told me to move on."

"Onto Gil?"

"No, just to move on, but—" The look of realization crosses her face. She failed her test of loyalty. "I won't give up on you."

I barely register Raya's movements as she unzips my pants with trembling fingers, her determination blending with her shame as she pulls my cock out and takes me into her mouth. I let her have her way, indulging her desperate need to reclaim a sense of control. I understand why she married my brother Gil; security is her sanctuary. But in the depths of my soul, I know her better than she knows herself. Raya despises feeling unfulfilled, and I relish the idea of tormenting her, a cat playing with a mouse that refuses to accept its fate.

My breathing gets heavy, and I tangle my fingers into her hair, controlling the motion. When I feel that tingle, I yank her head up. Raya opens her mouth wide, but instead of letting her swallow it, I bust all over her face.

Adjusting myself, I stand, looking down at her with a smirk that is equal parts satisfaction and contempt. "Now leave," I say, the cruel reality dripping from my words like poison, aware that in this game of love and betrayal, only one of us can truly win.

Chapter 40

Lana

I change into silk pajamas and unwrap my hair from the towel, letting it fall over my shoulders. A clean-up crew is disposing of all the bodies, and the announcement of his father's death will be shared tomorrow, spreading that he passed away in his sleep. As I brush my hair, there's a knock on the door.

"Lana, I know you're in there." Bianca sounds kinder than usual.

"Come in."

This is the first time I've seen Bianca look so disheveled. Her mascara runs down her face, her eyes like a racoon, and her stride of confidence is gone. She takes the hairbrush from my hand and begins to brush my hair.

"Bianca..." I urge her to speak.

"My mother would comb my hair anytime I'd see or hear something I wasn't supposed to. It always calmed me down. What did your mother do?"

I shift in my seat, unsure how to take Bianca trying to connect with me.

"My mother wasn't the most kindhearted."

"I can't imagine getting through life without my mother. My father on the other hand, I was never able to connect with."

Is she here to threaten me? Can you be beaten to death with a hairbrush?

"Bianca, I had to pick. It wasn't personal."

"I know." She continues brushing my hair. "I guess what I'm trying to say is...you could have killed Gil and had my mother killed. I would have lost my mother and brother on top of my father. Instead, you were going to use your bullet on the enemy. Thank you."

"Does this mean I gain your trust?"

Bianca lets out a light laugh. "You're getting there." She hands me the hairbrush. "I'm going to check up on mom, then lie my head down. You don't mind that we stay?"

"This place is big enough to hold a lot more. Plus, I think Adrian could use his family right now. He was close with his father."

She inhales and nods her head. "Before he got sent away, they were attached at the hip, but it was different when he came home. Everything was." Walking toward the door, she says one last thing before she leaves, "Lana, be kind to him. Out of anyone, he deserves it the most."

Chapter 41

Adrian

I see Bianca leaving my room as I approach the door, her expression weary yet resolute. "How is she?" I ask, concern tightening my chest.

"She's shaken up but holding out well," Bianca replies, her voice steady but lacking its usual spark.

"Go get some rest. You need it."

I nod, stepping into my room, where I find Lana lying on the bed, staring blankly at the ceiling. The moment she hears me, she sits up, her eyes widening with concern.

"Adrian, your face." She jumps out of bed, rushing toward me, her hands instinctively reaching for the bruised side of my face. Despite the pain, I let her touch me, the warmth of her hands contrasting sharply with the cold reality of my situation.

"Gil still punches like a bitch," I manage to say, trying to lighten the mood.

The fire in her gaze ignites something deep within me—a flicker of hope amid despair. For the first time in what feels like an eternity, I can sense a connection between us, an unexpected thread of trust binding us together. The soothing sensation washes over me, rekindling memories of safety I have long forgotten, a feeling buried beneath layers of betrayal and pain. My mind wrestles with the notion of how she can extend such unwavering trust toward me, despite all that I have put her through, despite the abuse, both seen and unseen. I don't deserve her kindness. I don't deserve her trust, yet here she is, letting her light seep into the dark corners of my existence.

"Why did you risk shooting the enemy?" I ask as I search her eyes for the truth within her motives.

"We were dead either way. It was worth a shot at distracting him," she replies, her expression resolute.

In that moment, I realize she could have let any one of us die. She could have walked away and been free of my tormenting presence. Yet, instead, she took a risk and aimed at the enemy. She chose to help me, not out of obligation or for any gain, but because she genuinely cares. The revelation strikes me deep, occupying the hollow spaces my own family has left barren. They hadn't cared when I sat rotting in a prison, taking the blame for my father's actions; they hadn't shown me an ounce of compassion. But Lana, despite the brutality I have inflicted upon her, sees something still worth saving within me.

Tears prick at the corners of my eyes—tears I haven't allowed myself to shed in years. I can't wrap my mind around the depth of her empathy. It suffuses my being with warmth, urging me to confront my demons, to be the man she believes I can be.

"You could have let me go," I murmur, shaking my head as if to dispel the weight of her kindness.

She tilts her head slightly, her gaze softening. "I won't

abandon you. Not now. Not ever." Each word is a gentle hand on my heart, a promise spoken in a language I have almost forgotten.

"You don't have to worry. Ever."

"Your brother was going to take your life. What if he had?"

"Gil likes the spotlight but could never handle it." Taking her hands into mine, I kiss them. "If Gil ever becomes a threat, I'll have him locked up."

"How?"

"The knife I used on your parents, it's one of a kind. Jagged edges, blood stains still on the blade. Gil likes to collect souvenirs. Each weapon used to take down all my rivals, he has kept."

Lana's unwavering presence begins stitching my soul back together, confronting the darkness that has consumed me. For the first time, I feel the heavy chains of my past loosening their grip, as if the possibility of redemption exists—if only I can find the strength to reach for it.

"Why are you looking at me like that?" she asks, her brow furrowing in confusion.

"Like what?" I respond, feigning ignorance, though the truth presses hard against my chest.

A blush colors her cheeks like a sunset, sweet and warming. "Like you're ready to devour me."

In that moment, I reach out, cupping her face gently in my palm. I trace her cheek with my thumb, lost in the raw intimacy of the gesture. We are both still recovering from the remnants of chaos, yet I can't help the rush of desire that surges within me. The sight of her, so strong yet so tender, is sexy.

"It shouldn't be a surprise if I want to," I murmur, my

voice low and steady, laden with a mixture of want and urgency. "If you prefer, I can look away."

"I don't mind," she replies, her face aflame with the weight of her confession, vulnerability shimmering in her eyes.

With that fragment of truth hanging in the air between us, I pull her toward me, my heart racing as I close the distance. I kiss her with a ferocity that feels hauntingly like desperation, as if every moment may be my last. It is a kiss forged in the fires of pain and longing—a promise, a plea, an acknowledgment of everything we have fought against. As our worlds merge and explode around us, I know we are tied in ways neither of us fully understands, bound by trust and the raw, unyielding desire to come alive, together.

Chapter 42

Lana

Opening my eyes, the sun shines through the slit of a shade that isn't shut fully. Adrian's arm drapes over my body, holding me in place. Wiggling my way out of his grip is impossible, so I have to nudge him to get off.

"Mmm," he hums in my ear. "I want more."

His hand grabs my thigh, making me giggle.

"I'll make you breakfast." I kiss his nose.

"Pancakes," Adrian says and then rolls over, setting me free.

I wrap a robe around me and get myself to the kitchen, where I start pulling out ingredients.

"Oslo!"

The shout startles me.

"Oh, Lana." Raya stops in her tracks. "What are you doing?"

"Adrian wants pancakes."

"Just tell Oslo to make it."

"I prefer doing it myself."

She lingers in the kitchen as though she wants to tell me something.

"Anything on your mind?" I ask.

"You know," Raya begins, her voice smooth as silk, "I really admire you, Lana. Putting up with all this." She pours herself hot water from the kettle into a mug and dips a tea bag in to let it stew.

"It's not as bad as people keep suggesting."

"That's why you're the better match for Adrian. It's a lot easier with Gil—less pressure. Don't get me wrong, Adrian and I had something special. It's a shame it didn't work out." Raya stirs some sugar into her mug.

"You and Adrian?"

She pretends as though she thinks I know. "He didn't tell you? I'm so sorry. I shouldn't have said anything."

My grip tightens around the whisk in my hand, my knuckles turning white. Raya is the one who broke Adrian's heart—the person who changed the meaning of love for him. The air between us thickens, charged with unspoken jealousy.

"It's in the past, Raya. It's okay." I lie. This isn't okay.

Raya's gaze softens, just for a moment, before hardening. "I wouldn't say in the past exactly."

"What are you saying?" I ask for clarification.

"The last time we were intimate was last night." Picking up her mug, she takes a sip as she watches me turn red. "Remember this," she said, her voice low and dangerous. "I had him first. And maybe...I still do."

Oslo walks in completely oblivious to the situation.

"Can you boil me more water?" Raya demands Oslo. "I want the kettle brought to the dining room table." As she turns to leave, she shoots me a wink.

When she's out of the room, I take the kettle from Oslo. "I'll take it from here. Don't worry."

I carry on making Adrian a nice breakfast, then place it on a serving tray and walk it to the room. When I get through the door, a smile crosses his face, and somehow that lights a fuse.

"You liar!" I shout, throwing the serving tray, spilling hot coffee onto him.

"What the fuck, Raya! I mean Lana! Fuck." Adrian is on his feet.

"She told me about last night."

Adrian's chest rises and falls at my words. "It wasn't like that."

"Oh no? Fucking her was like what then?!"

"We didn't have sex. I swear."

"But something happened."

He runs his hand through his hair in frustration. "She sucked me off. That's it. It didn't mean anything."

"I guess neither does this." I toss my wedding ring at him. "I can't believe you didn't tell me it was Raya." I storm out onto the balcony and inhale the crisp air.

Adrian comes up from behind me. "As though I don't look like a fool enough that I get out of prison, and my brother marries my fiancée. I don't need you to look at me differently." He grips the top of the railing with both hands.

"You don't know how I would look at you." I cross my arms against my chest. "Did it ever stop?"

"The last time I touched her was before I was locked up. Last night wasn't me giving in to temptation. It was to remind her I didn't want her. She was just another mouth I could shove my dick into. I know Raya, she's jealous of you. She regrets her choice, and I wanted to rip open that wound." He drops to his knees. "It meant nothing, Lana, I swear."

Watching him spiral out of character, my heart breaks into a myriad of pieces. The fire that once danced in his eyes is extinguished, replaced by a flickering sadness that makes him seem so small, so defeated. I have never seen this side of him—the tortured man beneath the monster. It's as if I am witnessing the final flickers of a powerful flame being snuffed out by guilt.

"I don't want her here."

"Then she will go. They can all go."

Suddenly, we hear pounding at the door with screams from the other side. "Adrian!" Hearing Bianca's voice, we both rush to open the door.

"What's wrong?"

"Raya." Bianca tries catching her breath. "She's not breathing."

Chapter 43

Lana

The soft hum of the funeral preparations dances in the background like a haunting melody. The layers of my simple black lace dress cascade around me as I stand among the Sokolov family surrounding the two caskets.

Bianca stands beside me in all black with a lace veil covering her face. She holds a tissue to her face to wipe her streaming tears. There is a pang of sorrow I feel for her as I know what it feels like to lose someone, multiple someones at the same time. My eyes are covered with large, dark sunglasses to hide my emotions.

"We gather here today in sorrowful remembrance of two vibrant souls whose time among us has been tragically cut short." The priest speaks slowly, allowing the words to float in the air for all to take in. "Today, as we say goodbye, let us also remember to honor the legacy our beloved has left behind. Rest in peace, dear Raya and Boris. You will be dearly missed but never forgotten."

I let out a soft sigh as the priest concludes the ceremony. Across from Bianca and I, on the other side of the casket, stand Gil and Adrian, the look of pain and anguish on their faces as they give their final farewell to a woman they both love deeply, adrift in their own oceans of sorrow. Gil stands with hunched shoulders, eyes glazed with tears that refuse to be contained, clutching a bouquet of baby's breath as the raw ache etches itself across his face. Adrian's expression is a mixture of deep sorrow and what looks like unvoiced regret compounded by memories of a woman he once cherished deeply. The tears streaming down his chiseled cheeks glisten with a pain that claws at my insides. We haven't spoken about Raya after I called him out. Will he always love her more? I watch as he bows his head as though grappling with the shackles of guilt, the 'what ifs' haunting him, the love he once felt for her is now put next to the reality that she will never return, leaving an aching void that threatens to consume him whole.

The jealousy I have harbored, like a festering wound, has finally been laid to rest with her passing; however, her spirit still lingers. Raya, the woman who had held my husband's heart in her hands, is a constant threat to me, and I feel consumed by the fear that her memory will always cast a shadow over my love. If I want Adrian to forget her, I have to give him all of me. Fully all of me. This isn't about love, it's about desire. Raw, unfiltered, and relentless.

Chapter 44

Adrian

The night sky is cool and balances the heat off my body as I sit on my balcony, drinking as I suffocate in my own thoughts yet again. Today is the strangest day of my life. I lost a woman I once loved with my entire being, yet I feel...a hollowness. A hollowness within me that holds all the emotions trapped inside. I'll miss the time we had together, but my love for her died the day she married my brother. She never loved me the way I loved her. Although it didn't surprise me that Gil went after Raya, I could never look at my brother the same after that. Gil has always gone after anything I have, want, or need. It has become part of his personality. He resents me being the heir to the Sokolov bratva.

"Penny for your thoughts?"

Lana comes walking in wearing a black lace thong and a black sheer lace bra that barely hides anything. I lean against the balcony, my hands to my side as I hold onto the top of the railing.

"I'm in no desire to play."

She pouts. "I see."

Lana has been distant the last three days, testing the waters.

"I don't want you to be upset. There's enough sadness around today. I lost my father and someone I used to really care about."

"I understand." She turns to walk into the bedroom.

"Do you?" I question following her.

She grabs a silk robe and puts it on. "I'll never be able to compare to her—she got the best of you."

"I don't know what you want from me, Lana."

With hurt in her eyes, she confesses. "Just you. I want to ruin your taste for other women, not because I give you my body, but because no one else speaks your language the way I do."

"You don't understand what you're asking for, Lana."

"I know exactly what I'm asking for, Adrian." She walks up to me and grabs my hands. "I want to feel your hands shaking because of me, not because you are unsure, but because I'm finally the woman worthy to stand by your side." Lana's expression is a mix of determination and hurt.

"You are Lana. You are worthy. You proved that."

"That doesn't seem to be enough, Adrian. I want your whole self. The broken parts, the scared parts, the beast, the boy, the man, the king. Let me see it. Let me love it. Let me own it." Lana remains desperate to be heard.

"You can't handle my peace and my madness, my softness and my storms. They come together, you don't get to choose."

"I don't want to choose."

Lana wants me to fight for this, and there's nothing more that I want. I'm willing to fight for this love, this internal war of trust, this longing to heal. I need to be strong enough to open my heart to her. This relentless, beautiful, gritty, chaotic life we are building together.

She wraps my arms around her, her presence filling the space between us. "I'll jump into every storm with you. We can make it work if you allow us to."

The sincerity in her words strikes me to the core, and I feel my defenses slipping. Each feeling I have been suppressing begins to bubble to the surface, leading to confusion and fear. If I just cast the fear aside, I will become hers entirely.

Chapter 45

Lana

Adrian looks at me, and I can almost swear he wants the same thing, but instead, he removes my arms wrapped around him.

"I'm traveling to Latvia for a meeting. I'll be back tomorrow." He kisses my forehead and walks out of the room.

I grab something off the nightstand and throw it across the room.

Shutting the balcony door as gray clouds invade the sky, I watch rain beat against the glass in a frantic rhythm, mirroring the chaotic thoughts swirling in my mind. I watch as droplets stick to the glass and slide down, blurring the edges of the world outside, just as my heart has blurred the line between love and hatred for Adrian.

Adrian—the man who has thrown me into a world of fear and uncertainty, yet ignites emotions in me that I haven't thought possible. He is both my villain and my savior. Panic twists my stomach when I relive the way he pulls me close, the warmth of his body against mine, the way he fights for me in his own twisted ways. It tears me apart to acknowledge it, but I want all of him. I want to be the one he desires, the one who can bring light back into his shattered existence.

Yet, the reality is suffocating. Adrian has walls around his heart—thick, impenetrable barriers built from past betrayals and buried anguish. Each time I gaze into those dark depths, I encounter not just the man I crave, but a man tormented by his own demons. Will he forever be trapped between survival and vulnerability? My gaze shifts to a reflection of myself in the glass—a mix of anger, passion, and an inexplicable tenderness. Rage courses through my veins— the kind that manifests as a burning desire not just to break through Adrian's defenses, but to incite a reaction within him, a relentless force that will drive him to realize I'm everything he needs.

I find myself walking toward my jewelry box and taking out the heart chain necklace. Lost in thought, a sigh escapes my lips as I try to shake off the worry clinging to my thoughts like shadows. Just as I walk toward the dresser to change out of my robe and lingerie, the bedroom door bursts open with a loud bang, the sound echoing as adrenaline surges through my veins.

For a fleeting moment, I can barely see who stormed into the room—figures cloaked in darkness, movements quick and purposeful. My heart races, instincts kicking in as fear claws at my throat, every nerve on high alert.

"Help!" I call out in panic.

They charge toward me regardless of my cry, body language aggressive, intent on subduing me. I stumble back, still clutching the necklace tightly, its weight suddenly feeling like a lifeline.

"Get her!" one voice shouts, deep and menacing, as

shadows play across the walls. Before I can react, their hands shoot out, grabbing my arms with a vice-like grip, dragging me back toward the door.

"No! Get off me!" I yell, panic rising in my chest as I struggle against their hold.

My heart pounds so loudly as I kick, twisting and squirming, desperately trying to break free. For a brief second, my thoughts flash to Adrian—his protective nature, the promise he's made to keep me safe. But momentarily, those thoughts are drowned by the sheer terror that engulfs me.

Suddenly, a second figure appears, their face obscured by a hood, and the cold, unyielding glare of a weapon emerging from their waist sends a jolt of raw fear through me. "Move it!" the voice commands harshly as something is put over my head. Everything is black.

They yank me down the hallway, the walls marching past in a blur. The cloth covering my face creates more panic, as now I am unable to see. With each stride, I feel the darkness creep in around me, cold and suffocating, a nightmare unfolding far too quickly. The cold air hits my skin, alerting me that we must be outside. A car door opens, and I am tossed in. Once the door is shut, the vehicle begins to move.

"If you move, I will blow your brains out," a calm voice says as the cloth over my head feels like it's suffocating me.

It isn't long before the vehicle comes to a stop.

"Out!" a man demands as a pair of hands yanks me out of the vehicle and onto my feet.

I walk with the cloth still over my face, being pushed in the direction of my kidnappers. A pair of hands grabs me again and practically drags me up a few stairs. I can feel cement under my feet until we proceed forward, and the cement is replaced with carpet. Continuing to be pushed in a particular direction, eventually, I feel the sole of a shoe against my back as I fall forward.

"Here she is," the man's voice says with triumph. "It was too easy."

The cloth is removed from my head, and a gush of fresh air envelopes me. When I look up, I see Gil.

"Hello, Lana."

Chapter 46

Adrian

The Queen of Spades that I planted worked flawlessly, creating paranoia. Since getting out of prison, I've felt a sense that there is this insidious betrayal lurking within my inner circle. I knew my father was looking to get rid of me, so he had to be the first to go. Part of me was in denial that my father would get me thrown into the Black Dolphin, hoping I'd meet my despise in there after I took the blame for his charges.

Driven by a fierce need for answers and fueled by this simmering rage, I embarked on a risky gambit. The plan included the raid, killing my father without having my family hate me for it, and the Russian roulette to see in a moment of fear who would be the hardest target to take down with no strings attached. It is a dangerous mission, a suicide mission, some may say, but the stakes are too high to ignore. This isn't just about securing power; this is about understanding the magnitude of the threat from those around me and neutralizing it before it completely destabilizes my position.

"We got a slight problem." Ivan walks to me as he updates me with an urgency threading through every syllable. "Border patrol ceased the shipment coming in from Ukraine. I'm looking into it, but at this point, I say blow it up and cut our losses." He crosses his arms tightly, as if physically holding back the weight of the situation.

Ivan is already on edge, given that he is against the meeting from the start, but without good reason, there's no reason for me to reconsider. This meeting will solidify the transportation of products further into Europe. Now that there's an issue with shipment at a border we are nowhere near, just further ignites my disapproval. My boy shifts from relaxed to alert.

"Where's Sergei?"

"Right here," Sergei's voice cuts through the air just as he steps into view, his expression a mix of defiance and frustration, eyes darting between Ivan and me, gauging the atmosphere.

"How did that shipment get stopped? That is the third one this month," I press with a steely tone as I take a few steps close to Sergei to further assert my authority.

"Like I said, new border patrol officers. I can't control that," Sergei replies with a hardened expression and an almost defensive posture.

My presence looms over him. "Your job is to get in control of it." My voice is edged with dissatisfaction, eyes narrowing.

Just then, my phone rings, interrupting the escalating tension. With a quick motion, I pull my phone from my pocket, glancing at the caller ID.

"Bianca, now's not a good time," I answer tersely with a mix of irritation.

"Make it a good time."

With a clenched jaw, I remind her, "There better be a good reason why you're disrupting me." My words laced with a warning as my calm demeanor begins to fray at the edges.

"It's Lana." Bianca blurts out. "She's...gone."

"What do you mean gone?" my voice drops low, simmering with intensity.

"I came to check up on her, and the house is empty. Barely any guards."

Blood rushes to my head, heat flooding my vision. I know just how reckless my brother can be. "Who was the last to see her?" Hate spews out of my mouth as though it's her fault.

"I don't know. What do you need me to do?"

"I'll send Sergei there to take care of it. In the meantime, just lie low."

I hang up the phone and turn to Sergei and Ivan, giving them commands. "Ivan, we need to speed this up. Sergei, I need you to head back to Moscow." My words fall heavily, thickening the room's energy.

"This meeting is important," Sergei urges, stepping forward, hands gesturing animatedly to emphasize the importance. "It took me a long time to get these connections going."

"Lana is missing." The words are caught in my throat. "I need you to investigate. Once this meeting is over, we are heading right back."

Sergei nods hesitantly, recognizing the shift in priorities and darts off before my focus lands back on Ivan.

Ivan steps forward, his brow still furrowed in concern.

"There's no way anyone would have gotten through. I made sure extra men guarded the property."

My jaw tightens against the gravity of the moment, sinking deep as I process the intertwining threats, a world of betrayals swirling around me, each decision heavy with consequence.

"I think we have a leak."

Chapter 47

Lana

Gil stands in front of me, and it's the first time I've seen him so out of character. Usually clad in perfectly tailored designer clothing, he stands there in a loose T-shirt and pajama pants, his grief etched deeply into his features.

"Sorry, I didn't mean to scare you," he says, his voice soft, filled with an uncharacteristic vulnerability.

Trying to steady my breath. "Why am I here?"

Holding out his hand for me to take, Gil's reply has a hint of playfulness in his tone, though it barely masks the sorrow lingering just beneath the surface. "I guess I'm just lonely. Not having my wife here, it's suffocating me."

Cautiously, I take his hand and get to my feet, gripping the robe around me even more. "You could have just asked me."

A shadow of sadness crossed his face, his eyes briefly clouding. "Adrian wouldn't like that."

"I wouldn't have minded making you some dinner."

Trying to inject some lightness into the tense moment. "I don't think he'd like knowing you kidnapped me."

"I know, I wasn't thinking straight."

I see the bottle of wine empty beside a wine glass, so I understand to tread carefully.

"I know how tough today was for you."

A shadow of sadness crossed his face, his eyes briefly clouding. "Does it get easier?"

"Grief is a funny thing. It comes and goes when it wants. You don't really have control over it—you just learn to live with it."

"Can I pour you a glass of wine?"

I hesitate a moment. "Water is fine," I say, forcing a smile.

Gil walks over to his mini-sized wine fridge placed in between shelves on the wall and uncorks a bottle. Beside the wine fridge is another mini fridge in which he pulls out a bottle of water. He takes an empty wine glass that is hung overhead and pours the water into it before handing the drink to me. Grabbing my glass, I take small sips, nervously aware of the tension hanging in the air.

"She was jealous of you," Gil speaks abruptly, his tone shifting to one of seriousness.

"Who?" My curiosity piques.

"Raya."

"Of me?" I shake my head incredulously while standing in front of him, clenching the tie of my robe. "I don't know how. She was a rare beauty; I could never compare."

"Well, you had something she didn't," he replies, his gaze steady.

"What would that be?" I inquire, my heart racing.

"Adrian."

The air leaves my lungs at his words. I glance around;

only the guards outside the room stand between us and utter silence.

"Gil, Raya loved you," I whisper, desperation creeping into my voice.

"Not the same way she loved Adrian." A bitter laugh escapes his lips. "Everything was magical until Adrian returned. He wasn't even angry; he accepted it, and I thought I'd won the girl back."

"Won the girl back?"

"Adrian never told you? Raya and I were together first. That's how they met. At some point, they fell in love."

Gil falls silent. His gaze sets on the wine bottle, his grip tightening. I place a hand on his shoulder, feeling his tension seep through the fabric of his shirt. Slowly, his grip relaxes.

"It's very possible she loved you both. But in the end, she chose you to spend the rest of her life with."

Gil nods.

"Let's toast in her honor," I suggest.

"To Raya," Gil says, raising his glass.

I delicately sip my water, feeling the weight of the moment. Gil downs a good portion of the wine from the bottle.

"I wish there was something I could say to make it less painful."

"You don't have to say a word," he replies, his lips curving faintly. Stretching his arm out toward me, he lifts the cup back to my lips, urging me to drink. "Raya would have enjoyed this moment." His hand lingers on mine, and half of the water is now down my throat.

Pulling away, I attempt to get out of his range, but the room begins to spin.

"What's going on?" I slur, confusion flooding my senses.

Falling to my knees, I try to crawl away, but my body betrays me, turning heavy and unresponsive. I see Gil's shadow loom above, his silhouette becoming menacing as I realize he spiked my drink somehow. The cup. The inside of it must have been laced. Dread washes over me as I fall forward onto my face, and he flips me onto my back and rips open my silk robe.

"Do you know what it's like having a spouse in love with your sibling?" Gil's voice cuts through the haze, filled with an anger I have never seen from him. He draws closer, kneeling beside me, pulling something shiny from his pocket. I can barely make out the knife amidst my fading consciousness.

"Gil," I beg, desperation pouring from my lips, hoping to reach whatever humanity remains in him.

The room spins violently, and I fight to stay awake as his skin brushes against mine, the cold blade of the knife ripping through my lace lingerie with ease.

"Five years in prison, and still I heard her call out his name in her dreams," he continues, his voice dripping with rage as he undresses me.

Tears stream down my face, helplessness consuming me as he continues to speak, my consciousness flickering like a faulty bulb until everything goes black.

I jolt awake, panic surging through me, ready to fight Gil off, only to find I am alone, naked, and confused on the floor. My head throbs painfully. I curl into a ball, gasping for breath, trying to find some semblance of control amidst the chaos.

"Finally, you're awake," Gil's voice slices through the silence.

Trembling, I curl tighter. When he appears before me,

he looks freshly showered and dressed in his usual attire, the stark contrast to the nightmare of how he appeared initially. He offers me a cup of water and Tylenol, but I turn them away, nausea rising.

"Fine, stay with a headache," Gil shrugs, placing the items on the table. "Adrian won't be back until tonight."

Tonight? I glance at the window, realizing the sun is high in the sky. I was here all night. My torn garments lie nearby, and I wrap my silk robe around myself, a weak attempt at being modest.

"Was that fun for you?" I spit, my voice a mix of anger and disbelief.

"It was, until you passed out. I still managed another two rounds," he replies nonchalantly, shrugging as if the horror of it all is trivial.

"Gil!" Bianca's voice pierces the thick air.

Fear shoots through me, and there isn't time to hide. Bianca walks in, her eyes widening as she takes in the scene —me, vulnerable and exposed with him, composed and confident.

"Lana, you should leave," she demands, her voice firm, a shield instinctively forming around me.

"It's not what you think," I implore, tears making my vision blur.

Bianca approaches with compassion, wrapping her arms around me. "I know," she says softly. "Let's get you home."

Her kindness envelopes me, but a chilling realization settles in my chest. This isn't the first time Gil has crossed this line. As we leave, Sergei is approaching us. He doesn't need to stop and ask, with one glance toward me, he pushes forward and enters the room where Gil is.

Bang.

Chapter 48

Adrian

In the heart of the arid desert, under a relentless sun, the skeletal remains of an abandoned warehouse stand sentinel against the horizon. Dust swirls like ghosts around the cracked concrete, and as the golden hour settles in, shadows elongate, casting an eerie glow. Inside, the atmosphere crackles with tension.

I stand tall, my posture relaxed yet alert, clad in a tailored black suit. Ivan stands slightly behind me, arms crossed, muscles tense, exuding a constant readiness. My sharp, calculating gaze scans the group of dealers before us.

Vik, part of the Morozov Family outside St. Petersburg, a wiry man with slicked-back hair and a crooked smile, gestures at a map as he lays out plans to move shipments through Western Europe. "We move underground by train," he asserts, his eyes glistening with excitement. "This will resolve the border issue for all of us."

I nod thoughtfully, feigning interest. My mind races, peering into the undercurrents of the meeting. I catch Ivan's eye; a silent communication passes between us, a shared awareness of the rising stakes. With confident smoothness, I lean in, tilting my head slightly as if contemplating the offer, but truly, I am dissecting every detail.

"How do I know this will be safe?" I question.

"Only one family from each region will have access to the railroad."

"How do you decide who is the lucky one?"

The man politely laughs. "It's survival of the fittest. You're dominating Russia, which is a huge area. Not only will this solidify your power and a heavy amount of cash flow, but you will have both Europe and Asia's attention at your command."

I exchange a quick glance with Ivan, who is already tense, suspicion etches across his face. With a barely perceptible nod to Ivan, he shifts slightly, a silent acknowledgment that this is about to take a turn.

I shift my weight, straightening slightly, my demeanor shifting from relaxed to imposing. "I appreciate the offer," I say calmly but edged with steel, "but I think it's best we take a step back." The warehouse falls silent, eyes widening, an almost tangible confusion amid the murmurs of disbelief.

Vik's smile falters, revealing a flash of irritation. "What do you mean, Adrian? This is the opportunity—"

"Opportunity to allow different families from all over Europe and Asia to invade my Russia."

"It will solve your shipment issues. The borders are only becoming stricter by the day."

"I have ships." I also have planes, but it's never wise to divulge extra information.

"Traveling by Sea takes too long. And most items get lost at sea."

That is an odd comment for him to make. Nothing truly

gets lost at sea; it's typically dumped into the water for a smaller-sized boat to pick up the packages.

"How often does the train run?"

"Once a week," Vik replies.

"How did you manage to build an entire railroad underground without being caught?"

I notice a nervous twitch in his jaw, and he seems to swallow hard, uncertainty flickering in his eyes. "When you know the right people," he smiles.

Stepping closer, I look him dead in the eyes. "What other families have agreed?"

"We plan to throw a soiree so everyone can introduce themselves. It's a great way to network and make friends."

"I don't need friends."

"The people around you are dropping like flies. I think having some friends will help."

"We do fine on our own."

"It could have saved your father."

The tension thickens like the air before a storm. Saved my father? There was no saving him. It was all part of my plan. I staged the Queen of Spades cards and the raid so it would look like an enemy took his life instead of his own son. This spares me having to deal with any grief from my mother and sister. Not even Ivan or Sergei know of the plan. Which means one of them is working against me, and this meeting is a setup.

I play along. "We are still looking for them. They will pay."

"We can help with that if needed."

"I'm sure you can."

I can see the dealers trying to mask their growing panic beneath forced grins, each one now calculating their next move.

Vik claps his hands once and rubs them together. "So what do you say? We have a deal?"

I extend my arm out and give him a shake. "It will be a pleasure dealing with you."

As he fishes his phone out of his pocket, I exchange a quick glance with Ivan, who stands just behind me, arms relaxed yet alert, carefully observing the men with a depth of scrutiny. My gut twists with anxiety, and I can't shake the unsettling feeling that one of my own is betraying me, but who are they working with? Is Sergei in on this? Is Ivan in on this? Or are they both mere pawns in a larger scheme?

I watch Vik dial a number, his eyes darting nervously, and wait for an answer. When he finally lifts the phone to his ear, my instincts kick in, and I move, taking hold of the device with a tight grip, curiosity and suspicion bubble in my stomach.

"Hello," I answer firmly, taking control of the conversation.

"Mr. Sokolov," a woman's voice responds, cool and calculated, devoid of emotion.

"Who has the pleasure of wasting my time today?" I shoot back with a mixture of sarcasm and disdain.

"I don't play around with money," she retorts.

"Neither do I."

"So, we have a deal? We can get our first shipment out this week."

I glance sharply at Ivan, gauging his reaction as he waits for a signal.

"Today," I demand. "I'm not here to waste anyone's time."

"Today then, give Vik the details."

Chapter 49

Lana

Lying in the warm water, the scent of lavender rises as I gently move the bubbles around me. This isn't the first time I've been raped, but this feels very different from the other times. I've always done so well with blocking them out, but I still feel Gil on me and in me. Bianca walks in and sits on the floor beside the tub, handing me a washcloth. There is a comforting yet chilling silence.

"You don't have to be here," I comment in a low voice.

"You shouldn't be alone." Bianca bows her head in shame. "No one should after something like that."

"Has he...to you?" I ask, unsure if I want to know the answer.

"No," Bianca shakes her head. "But he won't do that to you again."

"He might be dead physically but not mentally," I conclude.

"I'll make some tea. Do you want some?"

Sitting up in the tub, I say, "No, I'm fine. I just want to be alone."

She nods and gets to her feet. "You'll survive this, Lana."

"Oh, Bianca," I jolt up in the tub. "I wouldn't have any tea. They are all bad. Oslo got so sick from the last batch."

"I guess coffee it is."

Leaving me in the tub with my thoughts swirling in my head, I embrace the silence around me. Eventually, I get out of the tub, grabbing a towel to wrap around me. The steam still lingers in the air of the bathroom as I emerge from the tub. My hair cascading in wet waves, cheeks flush from the warmth of the water, I drape my body in a plush white towel. The soft fabric against my skin is like a warm hug that I desperately need.

I stand in front of the fogged mirror, the cool tiles beneath my feet grounding me momentarily as steam swirls in the air. The scent of lavender lingers, but it is no longer soothing. Instead, it twists with the distant echoes of laughter—a sound that has morphed into something sinister in my mind. My heart races erratically as I catch a glimpse of my reflection, my own face unrecognizable through the haze.

Wrapping the towel tighter around my trembling body, I try to shake off the wetness from my hair, but each movement feels more cumbersome than the last. Drops sliding down my body are somehow felt in my throat. The flash of memories invades my thoughts: Gil's grin, the way he had cornered me, the feeling of my world tilting off its axis. I can still feel the roughness of his grip, the helplessness that seeped into my bones as if I were conscious the entire assault.

My breath quickens, each inhalation sharp and shallow

as panic claws at my chest. It's as if a vice is tightening around my ribs, squeezing tighter with every beat of my racing heart. I press my palms against my sides, seeking some vague comfort that only comes with the pressing of flesh. I'm in the privacy of my own room, yet it feels like a prison.

Breathe. I encourage myself, but the words echo mockingly back to me, drowned out by the pounding of my heart in my ears. Images replay on a relentless loop: the smell of the leather sofa, the feel of the floor beneath me, the weight of last night colliding with the present. My hands tingle, an unwelcome sensation creeping up my arms, spreading like wildfire.

Suddenly, the air feels thick, suffocating. I bite down on my lip, hoping it will ground me, but instead, another wave of dizziness floods me. What is happening? The towel slips slightly, and I clutch at it, feeling exposed, vulnerable. The walls seem to close in, and the room twists around me. I am trapped in a nightmare from which there is no waking.

"Lana!" Adrian's voice echoes from outside the room, and I flinch at the sound. Reality collides with memory—a cruel reminder of what can happen, of what just happened. I can hear his footsteps, the rapid pounding of my heart echoing as he rushes toward me.

The door swings open, and Adrian stands wide-eyed, his expression shifting from anger to concern. The sight of him sends a pulse of warmth through me, but the panic somehow roars louder. I feel myself teetering on the edge, desperate for him yet terrified of needing him.

"Lana, look at me." His voice cuts through the chaos, instantly anchoring me, but I am still lost in the storm of my mind. My chest heaves, the towel slipping fully as I clutch at my bare skin, feeling more exposed than ever.

"I can't...I can't breathe," I gasp, each word a struggle, raw and jagged.

Adrian lifts me effortlessly into his arms in one scoop. "I've got you, I'm here," he murmurs, his voice a lifeline, piercing the suffocating darkness.

I lay my head on his chest with both hands gripping his shirt. His heartbeat through his chest becomes a soothing drum. With each breath he takes, I feel the panic begin to fade, the vice around my chest loosening just enough to let fragments of calm slip in. I close my eyes, leaning into him, the weight of the world beginning to fade as he holds me tightly, grounding me back to reality. Laying me down onto the bed, Adrian cuddles himself behind me, wrapping his large arms around my body, holding me to him.

"He's dead," is all I can muster to say. "I'm sorry."

I blink, still clouded by fear and the uncertainty of how Adrian will look at me now.

Adrian lifts himself onto his elbow and lets my back fall onto the bed. "What are you sorry for?"

I gulp. "Your father, Raya, and now Gil..." My mouth goes dry.

"Gil's days were already numbered, Lana. He just pushed up the due date." He traces his finger along my face. "I shouldn't have left you."

"I don't blame you."

"I've lost your trust," Adrian says with an intense gaze as he continues to cradle my face with gentleness.

"No," I reply in a whisper, "This isn't on you."

"I will fight with you, for you. You deserve to feel safe and loved."

The sincerity radiating from him begins to pierce through my heart. I feel a tear slip down my cheek.

"I love you," he declares. "You're all I have been

thinking about since the moment I left you. It hit me earlier today. I thought I was going to end up back in prison, and it wasn't fear that ate at me. It was the thought of losing you."

A sob catches in my throat with a flicker of unguarded vulnerability. Are his walls beginning to crack?

"I don't want to lose you."

He places a kiss on the tip of my nose. "You won't. There's someone undercover, and I'm going to expose them. So I need you to pack your bag and head to the airport. I will meet you there. Can you trust me?"

I nod. "Who is it?"

"We'll discuss that later. Right now, pack your things. We are going to be lying low for a few months, but trust me, when we come back, we will be stronger than ever."

"Okay," I reply.

"Lana."

"Yes, Adrian."

"I love you."

Chapter 50

Adrian

I shut the door to the taxi and watch Lana drive off. My chest tightens as I leave her behind once more. This time, it's crucial for both of our lives. This feels like the last piece of a puzzle needed to confirm my place as bratva king.

"We need to go," Sergei says, approaching me as he tosses his cigarette to the ground.

Ivan revs the engine of the Bentley Bentayga.

"Vik and his team are heading to the location now," Ivan says once we're all in the car.

"This will be life-changing," Sergei states.

"As long as this operation goes smoothly," I reply.

We arrive at the location on the outskirts of the city, crates stacked high with illicit products. The atmosphere is tense yet charged with the thrill of this operation.

"History is about to be made," Viks says as we approach them.

I stand confidently near a large wooden crate with my arms crossed, a smirk playing on my lips. This is going to be one for the books. Ivan inspects one of the crates while Sergei checks another.

"When will they arrive at their destination?" I ask Vik.

"In a few days, you'll get a confirmation call upon arrival."

Pulling out my phone, I begin walking back to the car. Letting myself inside, I pull out the cellphone from my pocket and call the last person I spoke to.

"Mr. Sokolov," the woman's voice purrs through the phone.

"Madame Sasha Morozov. Everyone is in place."

"I hope I can trust your word to uphold your end of our bargain."

Rolling my eyes, I play along. "If everything goes smoothly, I'll make sure to give you an unforgettable night."

"Looking forward to it. I wouldn't mind if Gil joins as well."

"You'll see him soon enough."

Hanging up the phone, I remain seated in the car to watch the show. The last conversation with my brother replays in my head.

* * *

"There's a leak within your circle, Adrian."

"That's a bold assumption," I chugged the last bit of vodka from the bottle.

"I checked the cameras from the house. The people's faces were covered, but I had the license plate of the van that dropped them off. It's traced to Interpol."

"*Interpol?*" *I took a deep breath. "What were you and Father doing all this time while I was away?*"

"*He didn't want to listen, Adrian. You know he was stubborn with me.*" *Gil sat down holding onto his rib cage.* "*You broke 2 ribs, you know.*"

"*I don't feel bad. You wanted to kill me.*"

"*Adrian, no idiot would give their hostages a loaded gun. I took my chance. I had to make them believe what they wanted to hear.*"

"*You need to get Madame Sasha Morozov to guarantee protection.*"

"*She's a headache. The only time that woman will shut up is when my dick is in her mouth.*"

"*Well, during the time your dick isn't in her mouth, tell her I need clearance.*"

"*What are you planning on doing?*" *Gil's interest was piqued.*

"*Don't worry about it.*"

"*Well, what kind of clearance do you need?*"

"*Diplomatic immunity.*"

"*Jesus, Adrian. You just got out.*"

"*Can I trust you to do this?*"

"*Consider it done.*" *Gil stared off in the distance.*

"*Something on your mind?*"

"*What were you and Raya talking about?*"

"*Nothing, Gil. We barely said a word.*"

"*She still loves you.*"

"*It doesn't matter. She was yours first. I took her from you. She wasn't mine from the start.*"

There was always this internal guilt for doing this wrong against my brother, and I was done reliving the past. I thought Gil was, too.

"You love her, don't you?" he questioned. "Lana. I see the way you look at her."

"She's my wife, Gil. Of course I do."

"It's different. I see it in your eyes." He got to his feet. "I'm happy for you, brother."

* * *

Gil was his own biggest enemy, but when I needed him to come through for me, he never failed. This was the only reason I kept him alive for that long. I watch the train door open and out floods Interpol. I watch who gets defensive. Immediately, Ivan begins shooting away while Sergei points his gun at Ivan. Rage begins to boil within me as I witness my two most trusted men fall before me. Sergei is the leak, and Ivan is taking the fall. I hate that I have to do this to him. Ivan doesn't deserve it, but I need to know who is on my side. I can see Sergei mouth to Interpol, asking where I am, but no one seems to care. That's when he knows he's in trouble.

Sergei puts Ivan in the Interpol car's backseat and then gets into the passenger's side. I discreetly follow them until we are far enough from the others, and then I cut my car in front of them. The tires screech as they try to stop, and they do so just in time.

We all lock eyes through the windshield. Sergei's face goes pale, but before he can pull out his own gun, the driver shoots him right in the head. His brain splatters all over the window. The driver jumps out, then opens the door to release Ivan, who is confused, but once he sees me, he runs over and gets into the car.

"What is going on?" Ivan asks, upset.

"Sergei works for Interpol, and right now, we need to

get out of here. Once things settle down, we will be back in action."

"Interpol will be looking for me."

"You're safe. We have immunity, but for now, we still need to set a few things straight before we go back to Moscow."

"Whatever you say, boss."

Chapter 51

Lana

I sit on the balcony of my suite nestled in the mountains of Austria, the DAS EDELWEISS Salzburg Mountain Resort. The pages of "Anna Karenina" lay open in my lap as time ticks away in agonizing silence. I trace my fingers over the words, finding myself entranced by the tragic fate of Anna—a woman ensnared by love yet doomed by her circumstances.

"Anna chose love, but at what cost?" I muse quietly, the echoes of my own heartache resonating in my chest.

Like Anna, I too had once believed in a love that could conquer the world, yet here I am, tangled in a web of danger and uncertainty, waiting for Adrian to come for me. I flip the page, but my mind wanders. It's been five weeks. My thoughts drift to Adrian—his fierce determination, the tenderness behind those enchanting, knowing eyes. He had promised to protect me, to eliminate every threat that loomed over us. But with each passing day, my heart grows heavier, an anchor tied to my fears. Am I simply a pawn in this dangerous game, destined to fall just like Anna? My heart feels like it's bleeding out—when did my feelings for Adrian happen?

The sound of approaching footsteps interrupts my thoughts, my heart racing in sync with the thud of my pulse. Panic surges, but just as quickly as it comes, it dissipates when the balcony door slides open, revealing Adrian. I spring to my feet, my eyes wide with disbelief and relief.

"Adrian!" His name escapes my lips like a prayer, and in an instant, he crosses the balcony, enveloping me in his arms. The warmth of his body against mine dispels the coldness that has settled in my heart.

"You're safe now," Adrian murmurs, his voice a low, soothing melody.

I bury my face into his shoulder, inhaling the familiar scent of him—cologne mixed with the faintest trace of gunpowder. It brings me a sense of comfort amidst chaos.

"I thought you forgot about me," I breathe, pulling back to look into his eyes, searching for the truth in them. "I was so afraid you wouldn't...that I was just a casualty or something."

The flicker of pain in his gaze speaks volumes. "Lana. Nothing could keep me from coming to get you."

Tears brim in my eyes, but this time they are of relief, of love that transcends fear. "What happens now?"

Adrian cups my face, his thumb brushing away a stray tear. "Things are going to be...different. We are going back to Moscow and claiming our place as Russia's only bratva king and queen."

"How —" I begin, but he silences me with a gentle shake of his head.

"I have dealt with it all; those who threatened you are gone. It's just us now."

In this moment, as I lose myself in the depths of his eyes, all my fears melt away. It is as though a weight has been lifted, revealing a path that is no longer shrouded in darkness.

"You lovebirds ready to go?" Ivan pokes his head out.

"Let's go," Adrian says, taking my hand and leading me back into the room.

"Where's Sergei?" I ask.

There is an odd silence. Adrian clears his throat, "Interpol took him."

"Interpol? You don't think he will turn on you?" The fear rushes back into my chest.

"Sergei is an Interpol officer. He was sent in as a mole."

I look to Adrian in confusion. "How did they arrest him then?"

"Sasha Morozov and I made a deal. We have diplomatic immunity as long as Sergei takes the fall."

I step back and pull away from Adrian. "In exchange for what?" I exhale shakily.

I know exactly what Sasha would have offered Adrian, and the thought of them together is making me sick.

"In exchange that I not only protect her husband, the Prime Minister, but secure his title when he runs for President of Russia." Adrian steps closer to me. "Did you think it was something else?"

A weak smile breaks through. "Maybe."

Taking both my hands and kissing them. "I'm yours, Lana. No one else will touch me."

The look in his eyes tells me he means it, and now it's my turn to reveal my feelings.

"I love you, Adrian."

Epilogue 1

Lana

"Bozhe moy! Bozhe moy!" Moans escape my lips, each one slipping out like a sweet melody laced with desperation.

With an orgasm gaining momentum, I lift my hips instinctively, a primal urge flickering within me. My fingers trail down to my clit, desperate to push myself over the edge, urgency igniting every nerve.

"Does it not feel good?" His voice is low, teasing and coaxing.

I manage a smile, my breath hitching. "Of course, baby. I'm just feeling extra naughty today."

His grin widens, a flash of pride sparkling in his eyes. To protect his fragile ego, I tell a white lie. It isn't that I don't find pleasure with him, it's just rare, like a forbidden fruit. I hate ending on a note of dissatisfaction. Once my fingers make contact, more pleasure courses through me, and with a final tilt of my hips, the orgasm crashes over me like a tidal wave. A moment later, I feel him pull out, and the warmth of his cum spills onto my stomach.

Falling onto the bed beside me, he presses a soft kiss on my cheek. "Lana, you'll be the death of me," he whispers, his breath brushing against my ear.

I turn onto my side to face him, tracing my finger along the taut ridges of his chest, savoring the intimacy. "Do you love me, Bren?" I ask, the weight of the question sinking into the silence between us.

His gaze softens. "Of course. You know that, don't you?"

I take a deep breath, my heart pounding as I summon the courage to ask the nagging question that claws at my insides. "When can we be together?"

He shifts, tension creeping into his posture, the space between us suddenly feeling like falling into a dark hole. Our weekly meeting in this exclusive hotel started out as an affair, purely physical, but over the last two years, it has evolved into something more, at least for me.

"We are together. Right now." Bren takes my hand, kissing it, but his eyes give away his unease.

"You know what I mean," I press, desperation staining my voice.

Bren sits up abruptly, searching for his clothes with a frantic urgency. "Lana, you are married, as am I. We can't just leave our spouses. I have children..."

"What about us?" The emotional plea slips from my mouth even though I fear it will fall on deaf ears.

He returns to the bed, falling to his knees, desperation on his face as he reaches for me. "I can't be selfish, Lana. For my children, I have to think of them. If I leave, they will be devastated."

I place a trembling hand on my stomach, feeling the

gravity of our situation. "And what about this child?" I whisper, my heart racing as I reveal what I learned recently.

Bren's eyes widen, horror flashing across his features as he stands aggressively. "It's not mine."

"Of course it is," feeling the fierce outrage rise within me.

He shoves his legs into his pants, hands shaking. "You better say it belongs to your husband."

"If this child is born with blonde hair and blue eyes, Beau will know it's not his."

He pulls his shirt over his head, the fabric crumpling in his fist. "Then get rid of it. I will not claim that child."

"Bren." My voice is faint, and the hurt I feel is a deep pang of pain.

"Lana. You knew what this was. I shouldn't have let it go on this long. I'm sorry. Truly."

With shoes in hand, he storms out, leaving me breathless, betrayal echoing through my heart. I feel doomed. Beau rarely touches me unless he forces himself on me, and even then, he isn't stupid enough to fall for this kind of lie. Knowing he will beat me until I admit who the father is sends chills down my spine. He will kill him without hesitation.

There is no protector left. Bren was meant to be my escape, my lifeline. Yet here I am, another man who has failed me. My father mirrors Beau's tyrannical grasp. He abuses my mother and has never respected a woman's worth, passing down that vicious cycle carried out by generations. It is time someone breaks it. That someone is going to be me. As I move to the coffee table, I pick up the newspaper. The headline reads in large bold font: "ADRIAN SOKOLOV, BRATVA PRINCE, TAKES BLAME FOR FATHER'S CRIMINAL CHARGES."

Tossing the paper back onto the table, I head for the shower, trying to wash away my turmoil. Might as well soak up what I can from this hotel room before returning to my prison—all walls and chains. The article keeps gnawing at the edges of my mind, fueling a crazy plan. It feels like a stretch, but the more I consider it, the more viable it sounds.

What do I have to lose? My inheritance is going to Beau; my father believes women are meant to have nothing to their name. How can I escape an abusive hold while simultaneously protecting what is mine? Killing Beau is out of the question. I won't stand a chance in prison. As poor as my life has become, I know I won't survive there.

Reaching for my phone, I dial the only other person who has a vendetta against my father that wouldn't affect me. "Come to Krass Hotel. Room 721."

Within twenty minutes, a knock echoes through the room. If there is anyone I can trust to make this work, it is my half-brother. My father refuses to acknowledge him, having impregnated a prostitute around the same time my mother had me. When his mother passed, he showed up at our door, vulnerable and desperate for shelter, but my father coldly turned him away. I remember searching the streets, finding him, and making a promise to protect him. He didn't deserve the cruelty that life handed him, and we found solace in our secret friendship.

I opened the door, a smile breaking across my face, amplifying my hopes. "Sergei."

"Lana," he replies, stepping inside with an innocent concern. "Is everything okay? Did Beau hit you again?"

"No," I shake my head, forcing a smile. "How's the ministry?"

Pride swells in his posture. "I'm at the top of my class. Detectives are already waiting for me to graduate."

"That's amazing," I breathe, sincerity ringing in my voice.

"I owe all this to you. Thank you, Lana." A pause settles between us, heavy with anticipation before he dares to ask the question lingering in the air. "Why did you ask me to meet you here?"

I inhale deeply, steadying my racing heart. "I need to cash in on that, thank you."

"How?"

I feel the weight of my words, pressing down like iron chains. "I have a plan. It's...risky. I got you a new life. I need you to do the same for me."

His brow furrows in concern. "I'm willing to help in any way I can, but I don't know how you can escape your father's legacy. I'm a bastard child no one knows about, but you, you are a bratva princess."

"Princess is just a lavish title for me. I don't get any of the privileges a princess entails, and it's time for that to change."

"Lana, you're making me nervous," Sergei admits, pacing the room as he processes my words.

"Just hear me out..."

Thoughts spill from my mind like a flood, one woven with fear and hope. Sergei listens intently, but for a few moments, he says nothing. Finally, he pulls out a cigarette, the paper crinkling in his fingers.

Pacing again, he finally looks at me, determination igniting his expression. "If you really want to do this, I will help, but this needs to be executed perfectly. One mistake could cost us both our lives."

"I know."

"And you understand that Adrian Sokolov won't be an easy match."

"That's why I need your help."

He takes a drag from his cigarette, contemplating. "You can't pick another bratva?"

"Adrian's an easier target."

"What do you need from me?"

"I need you to plant the seed that his father set him up."

"That's a reach, Lana. He won't buy it."

"You have to create this idea of mistrust," I urge, grasping the newspaper. "He's taking the blame for his father. I can maneuver the situation to ensure he receives a life sentence."

"How is that going to help you?"

"Stay with me, Sergei. I know the judge who will take this case—that will guarantee Adrian a life sentence. Then I will leverage the Prime Minister to pull strings to get him out. By then, you will have graduated from the Ministry of Internal Affairs and become a police officer. You can join the division working to dismantle the bratva. You'll go undercover and make your way into his inner circle, guiding Adrian's decisions."

"Too many people are involved. This will blow up in our faces."

"If Adrian truly is a bratva at heart, anyone who participates in his downfall will pay dearly," I assert, determination flooding my voice.

The light flicks on in his mind. "You want him to do all the dirty work," he concludes, a slow smile creeping across my face.

"Exactly," I confirm. "The Sokolovs are pushing to take over Russia. Once Adrian is out, his first stop will be to confront the judge who sentenced him. He'll continue his mission to eliminate competitors, both allies and rivals."

"You think he'll spare your life, Lana? If I suggest he spare your life, my cover will be blown," Sergei argues, his eyes narrowing.

"Not quite. I've discovered my father's will. It states I can only access my inheritance through my husband. Once Adrian knows this, he will have no choice but to let me live and marry me. That inheritance will give him access to all the borders, not just in Russia but across most of Eastern Europe. He wouldn't be foolish enough to let that slip away."

"You're willing to bet on that?"

"With my life."

Sergei shakes his head, concern deepening the lines on his forehead. "Being married to someone like Adrian won't be easy."

"No, it won't. I'll need to prove my loyalty. At some point, arrange for me to get arrested. It must be for something substantial. When I refuse to turn on him, he'll see I'm on his side."

"He has a brother and sister," he cautions. "You need their trust as well."

"We'll take care of them if necessary."

Sergei comes to the realization of my true intentions. "You want to eliminate everyone."

"Only those who threaten my freedom and existence. If I can get Adrian to handle anyone who has crossed me will be a double win."

It takes some time, but I finally break through his defenses.

"Are you sure about this?"

I nod firmly. Is it better to be alive and lonely or dead and forgotten? What's the worst that can happen? My life has been stained with love's absence. My parents and husband are like specters. I won't miss their existence, but I'll be damned if they barre me from claiming what is rightfully mine: the Petrovi power. For three months, Sergei and I meticulously plot every detail, constructing an intricate scheme. What he doesn't know is that he too is a victim of this cruel plan. Two can keep a secret as long as one of them is dead. Not only will I not have to worry about him exposing me, but I don't want him having my inheritance either. After all, he is a bastard's child, and I plan to be the last Petrova standing.

I am fully committed to making this plan work. Once I have studied the Sokolov family enough to know how they think and move, I know I'll be ready. Either Adrian kills me, or maybe, just maybe, finds an unexpected kind of love.

Epilogue 2

Raya

"**N**ow get out."

Cum drips down my face, the heat of his words stinging more than the evidence of my betrayal. I brace myself for the familiar chill that spreads through me—Adrian's gaze colder than ice. I can see the deep hurt in his eyes, mixed with an anger that leaves me vulnerable. I betrayed him, and he will never look at me the same way again. The thought of his marriage to someone else twists the knife further, while his rejection feels like a life sentence.

"You're so cruel." I rise unsteadily, grabbing tissues to wipe my face, my hands trembling slightly.

"Let's not play that game. I'll call you things far worse than cruel." Adrian's calm demeanor only intensifies the anger bubbling beneath the surface, his eyes locking onto mine like a predator sizing up its prey.

My heart shatters, the sound echoing in my ears.

"Adrian, please hear me out," I plead, my voice trembling, but my words fall on deaf ears, swallowed by the silence of the room.

"I said, get out."

I don't fight for his attention; instead, I turn and leave, my feet feeling heavy as I step out of the room. Tears prick at my eyes, threatening to spill. What's the point? I'll never have his love again. He won't let me explain, doesn't want to hear the truth. But what good will it do? No one will believe the nightmare I endure.

Adrian can think I betrayed him, but I had no choice. I didn't marry Gil out of love. The night Adrian was thrown into prison, Gil came to comfort me, but his intentions were cloaked in darkness. I was drugged and raped as I fell in and out of consciousness. Each night was a mental torment I couldn't escape, and shame silenced my cries for help. When I fell pregnant, Gil's threats became a noose around my neck. *Marry me or I'll gut that baby right out of you.* So, I submitted to his will, even allowing him to plan our wedding on the date Adrian and I had dreamed of. The stress and grief of it all broke me. I lost the child, haunted by the weight of my choices.

As I leave the room, I find Gil leaning against the wall, his posture casual, but his presence chilling.

"What were you doing?" His voice is overly sweet, laced with an underlying menace.

"Nothing," I lie, biting my lip to hide the tremor of my breath, willing my sweat to dry.

"Who were you with?" His tone sharpens, slicing through the air.

I gulp, a lump forming in my throat. "I was alone."

Pushing off the wall, he moves toward me slowly, deliberately. "Raya," he sings my name like a soft threat, taunting me. "Why are you lying?"

A wave of nausea crashes over me. I know that admitting the lie would lead to punishment. If he finds out I lied, it will be worse. The abuse he inflicts isn't always physical; it's the mental games, the degrading, the confinement, the complete erosion of my spirit. When I wrote to Adrian that I was getting married, Gil had retaliated by shaving my head, stripping me of my dignity. His cruelty knew no bounds; just simply trying to engage in conversation with Adrian in the room was enough to set Gil off. When I asked Lana about their honeymoon, this caused Gil to gift our house in Cyprus to Adrian and Lana and make me watch them fuck all over the place.

"Gil, you should be resting," I say cautiously, brushing my fingers along his arm, searching for a moment of peace.

His ego, bruised from his earlier fight with Adrian, looms like a storm cloud just above us. He has always been overshadowed by Adrian's strength, and today is no different.

"I was resting just fine, waiting for my tea. I didn't know it took so long to boil fucking water, Raya."

"I couldn't find the tea. I'm sorry." The words slip out, my voice barely above a whisper.

When I hear footsteps coming from behind me, my heart stops.

"Gil." Adrian's firm voice slices through the atmosphere, his presence a dark shadow closing in. "We need to talk."

"Yes, we do," Gil replies sincerely, but his glare sends a jolt of terror through me. "Raya, my love, get to bed."

I nod, unable to move, my limbs feeling heavy with dread. Gil steps closer, placing a soft kiss on my cheek, but the intimacy is suffocating.

Whispering into my ear, he breathes, "You're dead."

As he strides toward Adrian, I manage a fleeting glance,

hoping to convey my desperation. If Adrian reveals our encounter, it will spell disaster for me.

The world starts to spin, my senses dulled as I grapple for stability. There's only one thing I need to do. I have acquired wolfsbane, planning to poison Gil, hoping to reclaim my freedom and find my way back to Adrian. But with the door to that hope now firmly closed, I resolve to use it on myself instead. The weight of despair settles in; I see no other escape.

Also by Marianna Buffolino

Fallacy - Entangled

Condemned

Condemned to You